GANG TACKLE

orca sports

GANG TACKLE

ERIC HOWLING

ORCA BOOK PUBLISHERS

Library and Archives Canada Cataloguing in Publication

Howling, Eric, 1956–, author
Gang tackle / Eric Howling.
(Orca sports)

Issued in print and electronic formats.
ISBN 978-1-4598-1225-3 (paperback).—ISBN 978-1-4598-1226-0 (pdf).—
ISBN 978-1-4598-1227-7 (epub)

I. Title. II. Series: Orca sports
PS8615.09485G36 2016   jc813'.6   c2016-900454-6
c2016-900455-4

First published in the United States, 2016
Library of Congress Control Number: 2016931867

Summary: In this high-interest sports novel, Jamal and his teammates take a stand
against their new coach when his bullying and discrimination go too far.

*Orca Book Publishers is dedicated to preserving the environment and has printed
this book on Forest Stewardship Council® certified paper.*

Orca Book Publishers gratefully acknowledges the support for its publishing
programs provided by the following agencies: the Government of Canada
through the Canada Book Fund and the Canada Council for the Arts,
and the Province of British Columbia through the BC Arts Council
and the Book Publishing Tax Credit.

Cover photography by Corbis Images
Author photo by Theo Wilting

ORCA BOOK PUBLISHERS
www.orcabook.com

Printed and bound in Canada

19 18 17 16 • 4 3 2 1

For Mr. Rothney, the best teacher I ever had.

Chapter One

The ball was snapped.

Jamal broke from the line and raced down the right side. He had to get in the clear. Find an opening in the defense where he could catch the ball. That's what the play called for. That's what a wide receiver had to do.

Jamal's legs churned and his arms pumped. His eyes were focused straight ahead. The yards disappeared under him one long stride after another. He blazed straight down the field.

The defender caught him. Carlos Lopez was the fastest safety Jamal had ever played against. He wasn't tall or powerful, but he was sneaky quick. He covered Jamal like glue and stuck to him step for step. Watched his every move.

Jamal cut to his left—a turn so sharp it surprised Carlos. He tripped and stumbled to the ground. Jamal was in the clear. He looked over his shoulder as the quarterback launched the ball. Darnell Williams had a gun for an arm, and the ball shot through the air like a bullet. A perfect spiral heading straight for his star wide receiver.

Jamal reached out his arms. He watched the tip of the ball sail toward him. The leather landed softly on his fingertips, and he squeezed tight. Then he tucked the pigskin under his arm and dashed down the field.

No one could catch him now. Not Carlos. Not Eli. Not Rico. He shifted into high gear as fifty yards flew by. He galloped across the goal line and raised the ball in the air. Touchdown!

Carlos came panting up behind him. "You were lucky, dude."

"You know you can't cover me." Jamal grinned, flipping him the ball. "I've got too many moves."

"I had you, but I tripped on that huge clump of grass." Carlos pointed to a large mound on the field. "This field sucks."

"Yeah, it's brutal," Jamal said, kicking some brown where there should have been green.

"Has been ever since the Saints got canned last year."

"Yeah, I still can't believe we're not playing," Jamal said. "Those budget cuts killed the football team."

"They could have cut the band or choir." Carlos shook his head. "But no, they whacked the football program instead. What were they thinking?"

"I guess they just ran out of money," Jamal said with a shrug. "It's not like we live in some flush part of Toronto. Just take a look around." He pointed his thumb over his shoulder. Southside was getting more and more scuzzy. Rundown apartment buildings like the one he lived in needed new paint. Some houses were vacant with windows boarded up. Old cars were parked on the street, some so dusty they looked like they'd been there for months. Garbage was tossed in the alleys, and bus shelters had graffiti spray-painted on them. None of it bothered Jamal though. He had grown up in Southside. This was his home turf.

"This should be the first day of practice," Carlos said. "A real Saints practice. With real uniforms, pads and helmets. And a real coach. Not six guys running around in beat-up kicks and jeans on some crappy field with over-grown grass."

Jamal and Carlos jogged back to where the other four players stood. Darnell Williams and Billy Chang were on Jamal's team. Eli Davis and Rico Bellini were on Carlos's squad. They were all friends— all seventeen years old. And they had all played on the Saints the previous year. Quarterback, center, wide receiver, backup QB, halfback and safety. They had most of the key positions covered. Now they could only play pickup football after school.

This was their first three-on-three game of the year. They had all just finished day one of their grade-twelve classes at Southside High. Or at least most of them had.

"Didn't see you in the halls today, Rico," Eli said.

"Hey, man, I was in the library studying all day," he said, grinning.

Billy burst out laughing. "You in the library all day? That's a good one. Do you even know where it is?"

"What's the point in me going to school?" Rico asked. "We all know I'm just going to end up like my old man. Dumping garbage into a truck every day. It's an okay job, but I don't need school for that."

"You never know, bro," Darnell said. "You might learn something you actually like. Besides, if my mom ever found out I wasn't in class...she'd kill me."

"Me too," Jamal said, his hand slicing across his neck like a knife.

"Let's go, brainiacs," Carlos called out. "Are we here to talk about school or play some ball?" He tossed the pigskin to Eli, who would be playing quarterback.

After Jamal's touchdown, the teams switched positions. Now Jamal was on defense. He lined up across from Carlos and waited for Eli to snap the ball to himself.

"Hup!" Eli shouted.

Carlos took off and sprinted straight downfield. Jamal knew he'd try to get back at him. He wanted revenge after giving up a touchdown. Jamal stuck beside him. He knew Carlos would try a move, so he had to be ready for anything.

Carlos cut to his right. Jamal thought he was heading to the sideline for a square out. He cut with him. But Carlos had a different pass pattern in mind. He turned upfield and headed for the goalpost. Jamal had been fooled, but only for a split second. He turned on the jets and raced after the tricky receiver.

Jamal looked back to check the quarter-back. Eli was about to throw. He cocked his arm and fired the ball downfield to Carlos. But his arm wasn't as strong as Darnell's. The pass wobbled as it floated through the crisp September air toward its target.

"I got it!" Carlos shouted.

"Don't think so," Jamal said, jumping in front of him at the last second.

Jamal picked off the ball and cradled it in his left arm. He stopped on a dime, switched gears, then bolted the other way. Carlos chased after him. Jamal knew he'd be mad. No one liked to be intercepted.

Eli and Rico waited for him in the middle of the field. Their arms were spread wide—all they had to do was touch him. That would count as a tackle, and the play would be over. Jamal had other plans. He juked to the right and blew past the two defenders. With nothing between him and another touchdown, he crossed the goal line and spun the ball on the ground to celebrate.

Billy reached his hand high. "Up top." Jamal grinned and high-fived him.

"I'm glad you're on my team, bro," Darnell said.

"Tomorrow we switch players," Carlos said. "I'm tired of Jamal making me look bad."

The friends fist-bumped each other before heading out. Jamal picked up his backpack and headed to the sideline. Out of the corner of his eye he noticed a green car in the parking lot. Someone had been watching him.

Chapter Two

Jamal walked toward the thumping music.
A rap track with heavy bass was pounding
out of the rolled-down windows. It was no
ordinary car. He thought it looked like a
classic Chevy, at least thirty years old. The
metallic lime-green paint on its hood sparkled
in the late-afternoon sun. The sides hung
extra low and almost touched the pavement. Suddenly the frame bounced up.
Then Jamal knew why—it was a lowrider.
He had spotted one or two driving around

the Southside streets, but he had never seen one up close.

He kept moving toward the car and glanced inside. Two men looked out from the front seats. The man on the passenger side opened the door and got out, waving for Jamal to come closer.

The man looked tough. His head was shaved bald, sunglasses covered his eyes, and dark stubble peppered his face. He was short, and burly like a bull. He wore a black tank top that showed off thick arms covered with tattoos—a dragon, a knife, a gun. Every square inch of his skin was marked with dark purple ink. He leaned against the old Chevy, his dark jeans on the green door, his leather boots on the black pavement.

Jamal watched his bicep bulge as he waved him nearer one more time.

"You're fast," the man said.

"Thanks."

"We could use a guy with your wheels."

Jamal was scared, but he didn't want to show any fear. He kept his face calm. He knew he had something the man wanted. Speed.

"What for?" Jamal asked.

"Little of this, little of that." The man crossed his arms and smiled.

Now that he was closer, Jamal saw another tattoo. *SS CREW* was inked on the man's neck. He had seen the marking before. He wished he never had. His father had the same tattoo needled into the side of his neck. It stood for Southside Crew. They were the biggest gang on the Southside.

Jamal knew they were into a long list of bad things, all of them against the law. Theft. Drugs. Gambling. Violence. He knew the last one could be deadly. His own dad had been gunned down in cold blood, killed by a rival gang as payback. The East Side Roaches had accused the SS Crew of stealing from them. His dad had nothing to do with the crime, but it didn't matter. Someone from SS Crew had to pay. And that someone was his dad. The memory was still seared in Jamal's brain. It had happened a year ago, but to Jamal it seemed like just last week.

"What do you say?" the man with the tattoo asked.

Jamal knew these guys were bad news, but still he was curious. "What's in it for me?"

"Money," the man said. "More money than you can dream of."

Jamal wondered how much. His mom worked a cash register at Best Buy. She made enough to put food on the table and pay the rent, but there was nothing left over. He worked flipping burgers at McDonald's two nights a week. He earned a few bucks for buying lunch in the school cafeteria, but not much more. He never had money for a new hoodie or kicks.

"How much money?"

"Ten large."

Jamal let out a low whistle. "That's a lot of coin."

"You know it, dawg."

Jamal imagined what he and his mom could do with ten thousand dollars. New clothes, a new TV, maybe even a new car. It could change their lives. He took a deep breath and tried to think straight. He knew getting involved with a gang was a mistake. It could only lead to one thing—trouble. But still.

"I'm not interested," Jamal said, shaking his head.

"You sure, kid?"

"I'm sure."

"If you ever change your mind, you know where to find me." He smiled for the first time, revealing a shiny gold tooth. "Just look for the car. It's one of a kind." The man climbed back into the lowrider. "Let's roll, Martinez."

Ice Cube started rapping again. The driver bounced the car up. He stepped on the gas and the engine growled. Jamal watched the Chevy pull out of the parking lot. He checked the license plate—*SS CREW1*.

Chapter Three

Jamal stretched out his long legs. He slouched at a desk in the back of his Language Arts class. Mrs. Cooper stood at the front. She held a small paperback in her hand and scowled at the students.

"Who's done their homework?"

The class was silent.

"Who's read the first chapter I assigned?"

No one raised a hand.

"Who's even opened the book?"

Still no answer.

Mrs. Cooper marched down the aisle. She came to a stop and crossed her arms. "Darnell, you look like a strong guy. Were you able to pick up the book? Or was it too heavy?" She waved the thin paperback around to show how light it was.

"I must have hurt my arm playing football." He smiled. "I wasn't able to lift it."

The teacher looked around the room. "Carlos...Eli...Jamal, how about you?"

Only Carlos spoke. "We all got injured playing ball as well."

"I didn't think we had a football team," Mrs. Cooper said, cyeing Carlos suspiciously.

"We don't." He raised an eyebrow and grinned. "But you know how rough touch football can be."

"And what about Rico? Isn't he supposed to be in this class?"

"Aah...I think he's sick," Jamal said.

Eli nodded. "Yeah, sick of school." Jamal, Carlos and the rest of the class all snickered.

Mrs. Cooper put her hands on her hips. "Well, if you're not going to read at home, then I'm going to make you read in class. Everybody get out your copy of *The Catcher in the Rye* and start reading. And I don't want any talking."

Jamal could hear the teacher muttering to herself as she retreated to her desk. He pulled the book from his backpack and turned to page one. He glanced to his right, where Carlos was sitting. He wasn't reading. He was too busy scribbling a note.

Carlos folded the paper and tossed it onto Jamal's desk. Jamal hid the note behind his book so Mrs. Cooper's hawk eyes couldn't see it. He opened the paper.

Big meeting in the gym after school.
Something about football. Pass it on.

Jamal folded up the note and tossed it over to Darnell. Then he went back to reading his book. Not much was sinking in though. His mind was on football. He wondered what the message meant.

Jamal cruised down the hall with Carlos and Darnell. The other kids moved out

of their way. Stayed close to their lockers.
They were three strong guys with reputa-
tions. No one wanted to mess with them,
not even the teachers. Jamal knew most of
the stories weren't true, but he wasn't going
to destroy his street cred by correcting them.
He just let people believe what they wanted.

The three rounded the corner and
walked into the gym. They bumped fists
with Billy and Eli, who were already there.
About twenty other players from last year's
team were packed together in a big huddle.
They were standing against the wall under
the GO SAINTS GO! sign left over from
last year when there was still a football team.

"Any news, Eli?" Jamal asked.

"Negative. They haven't started the
meeting yet."

"There's a rumor the team's getting
back together," Billy said excitedly.

How can that be? Jamal wondered.

The principal of Southside and the
Saints head coach from the year before
walked toward them. Principal Campbell
and Coach Kemp had been meeting in a

small office at the side of the gym. The principal was new to the school and still trying to make her mark. She was no nonsense and all business. Coach Kemp had run the Southside team for years. He was easygoing and knew football inside out. Jamal and his teammates loved to play for him.

"Listen up," Coach Kemp said, adjusting his ballcap. Jamal and his teammates put a lid on their conversation and moved a few steps closer. "As you all know, the Saints football program was canceled last year. We just didn't have the money in our school budget."

The players cupped their hands around their mouths and booed.

"But Principal Campbell has an exciting announcement to make."

"That's right, Coach." She held up her hands for quiet. "Yesterday I received a call from the president of Fort Sporting Goods."

Jamal knew all about Fort Sports. They were the biggest sports-equipment company in Canada and had stores all over Toronto. He often stopped by to check out all the cool football gear. Gear he could never afford.

"Mr. Fort is a big supporter of high school football, and he made me an offer. But before I said yes or no, I wanted to ask what you all thought."

"Lay it on us," Carlos said.

The principal cleared her throat. "Mr. Fort wants to donate twenty thousand dollars to Southside High to get the Saints football team going again."

The gym exploded with cheers and whistles.

"He's willing to give us all the equipment and uniforms the team needs."

"So what are we waiting for?" Darnell asked.

"There's a catch," Principal Campbell said, glancing around at all the players. "Mr. Fort also wants to be head coach."

"What about Coach Kemp?" Billy Chang asked. "He'd be the assistant coach, right?"

"I'm afraid not," Coach Kemp said, shaking his head. "Mr. Fort wants to coach alone. He says he has his own way of doing things."

The players groaned at the news Coach Kemp wouldn't be allowed on the team. But the players were still pumped by the news.

"Is there still time to play this year?" Jamal asked.

"I called the league and told them about our situation," Coach Kemp explained. "They said that if the team started practice right away, you could still play this season. The Saints' first game would be in two weeks."

"So, that's the deal," Principal Campbell said. "But like I said, I wanted to ask all you players first. I thought we could take a vote."

Jamal felt bad that Coach Kemp wouldn't be part of the team. But he would do almost anything to play on a real foot-ball team again. Playing pickup with his friends after school just wasn't the same. He knew Carlos, Darnell and the other guys felt the same way. If that meant letting some rich guy be coach, well, that was just the price they had to pay. *How bad could he be anyway?*

Principal Campbell raised her arm. "All those in favor of playing football this year?" Every hand in the gym shot up. "Wonderful! I'll call Mr. Fort and give him the good news."

Just at that moment the gym door swung open. In walked Rico.

"Looks like someone has made an amazing recovery from being sick," Carlos joked.

"When I heard there was a football meeting, I suddenly felt cured," Rico said with a smile. "Did I miss anything?"

"The Saints are back," Jamal said. "I'll fill you in."

Chapter Four

"Check out the new unis, man!" Rico's huge grin curved up like goalposts. He stuck out his arms to show off the new team colors. The uniforms were royal blue with white-and-gold numbers on the front and back. "With threads like these, I'm definitely coming back to school."

Jamal stood next to Rico in the locker room. He pulled his own jersey over his brand-new shoulder pads. He had never had new equipment before. For years

Southside had made do with gear left over from previous seasons. Jerseys that were ripped from too many tackles, helmets that were missing chin straps, pads that were so thin they wouldn't protect anyone. Last year Carlos had been hurt because his shoulder pads were too small. Wearing a new helmet, shoulder pads, pants and cleats made Jamal feel like he was in the big leagues. That he played on a school team that cared about football, like all the other school teams did.

"What's this?" Darnell asked, pointing to a colorful cartoon fort on his shoulder.

"It's the Fort Sports logo," Eli said. "You know, like the store."

Billy grimaced. "It looks like one of those blow-up bouncy castles at a kid's birthday party."

"We're the Saints, not the Bouncy Castles," Darnell said.

It didn't seem to bother Carlos. "If a bouncy castle gets us new jerseys and equipment, then I'm cool with it."

"Me too," Eli agreed.

The other heads in the locker room nodded. Still, Jamal wasn't so sure.

Suddenly the door to the locker room swung open. Jamal looked over and was almost blinded. Bright TV lights and camera flashes followed a crowd of people. It was a crazy scene. Reporters were shouting questions. Photographers were jumping over each other trying to get in the best position to cover all the action. Principal Campbell led the media crush into the middle of the room. Microphones were thrust in front of her as she began to speak.

"I'd like to have everyone's attention. This is a big day for Southside football. And none of it would be possible without the gentleman standing to my left." Principal Campbell nodded at the man beaming next to her. He was big, almost fat. Dark, stubbly hair topped a face that was red and round. Sweat beaded on his forehead. The black suit he wore had to be left unbuttoned at the front. It just wasn't big enough to cover his paunchy stomach. "I'd like everyone to meet the president of Fort Sports and the new head coach of the Southside Saints, Mr. Roland Fort."

Hoots, whistles and applause filled the locker room. Jamal and his teammates knew they wouldn't be getting to play real football if it wasn't for Mr. Fort.

"This is a great day for the Southside Saints and a great day for Fort Sports," Mr. Fort said, holding up a new jersey. He flashed the Fort logo in front of the cameras. "First of all, we can get rid of all that *president* and *Mr. Fort* stuff. From now on, just call me Coach."

Jamal liked that. Any coach should just be called Coach. But he did wonder why he only showed off the logo for Fort Sports and not the Saints.

"At Fort Sports we want to make sure every high school can have a football team. Even a school like this one." Coach Fort smiled for the cameras again. "That's why Fort Sports has donated twenty thousand dollars to get the Southside team going again." The crowd hooted and clapped again. "Now, if there are any questions, I'd be happy to answer them."

Jamal could see some of the reporters had questions, but so did he. A big one. He was nervous in front of all the TV cameras, but he asked anyway. "What do you mean, *a school like this one?*"

Coach Fort looked uneasy. He dabbed the sweat from his forehead. "You know, for kids and a school that are...disadvantaged."

Jamal had never heard anyone describe him as disadvantaged before. Poor, maybe. Having to work hard to get ahead, maybe. But disadvantaged? That sounded like he was beat before he started. He had never felt that way—on or off the football field.

"Let me explain," Coach Fort said. "I look around the room and I see kids with skin of all different colors. Kids that may not have a bright future because of that. Kids who may want to quit going to class. Who may be wondering *what's school going to do for me?*"

Jamal glanced at Rico. He was nodding. He hadn't gone to class the whole first week.

He didn't think school was going to get him a better job. Jamal thought Rico must be the kind of kid Coach Fort was talking about. But his other friends weren't like that. Darnell, Carlos, Billy and Eli might not like doing homework, but they all thought school would help them. They all had plans.

"Football is a great reason to come to school," Coach Fort said, grinning into the cameras. "Maybe it's the only reason you come to school. And you never know. If the Fort Saints—I mean, the Southside Saints do well, these kids might even get to play college or pro. Now that would be something!"

Jamal's eyes darted over to Principal Campbell. He saw her jaw drop. He could tell she wasn't happy with what Coach Fort was saying about their school, but it was too late. She had wanted a football team just like the players had. Saying yes to Roland Fort and his money was the only way to get one. All she could do for now was bite her tongue.

"Principal Campbell," a reporter said, pointing his microphone at her, "do you think football is a good reason for kids to come to school?"

"Playing football," she said, gritting her teeth, "is just one of many good reasons to come to Southside."

Jamal rolled Coach's words around in his head. What did he mean? That football was the only reason Jamal went to school? That he had no future because of his skin color? That he wasn't smart enough? Jamal wasn't sure he believed any of that. All he knew was that he liked to play football. And Coach Fort was giving him that chance. He couldn't wait to hit the field.

Chapter Five

"Now, who wants to play some football?" Coach Fort asked, pointing to the door.

The locker room exploded with cheers.

"All right!" Carlos shouted.

Billy punched the air. "Let's do this!"

"Go, Saints, go!" Rico cried.

Coach Fort marched the team outside like he was leading a parade. He talked into the microphones as the TV cameras followed beside him. "This is what I'm talking about, people. Look how excited the players are. Does going to class get them this excited? No way."

Jamal felt proud wearing his blue-and-gold jersey. But his uniform wasn't the only new thing at Southside. Thanks to the money from Fort Sports, the field had undergone a makeover too. Grass had been cut, bumps smoothed out, white lines marked every ten yards and stands painted. The Saints gridiron was ready for the first game of the season.

Coach stood on the sideline and said goodbye to the TV cameras and reporters. "As the president of Fort Sports, I want to thank you for being here today. And you're all invited back to see how I'm helping to give these down-and-out boys a future."

"*The Sports Channel* will be coming back every week," a reporter said. "TSC will follow the team. Cover each game. See how you're helping the kids. We're going to call the show *Saint Roland*. You know, like how you're saving the Saints."

Coach Fort beamed from ear to ear. Jamal could see he liked the sound of that.

The reporters packed up their cameras and microphones and went back to their trucks. Jamal and the rest of the team took the field.

Coach Fort called the players in. They surrounded him in a big circle at midfield. "The first game of the season is only a week away," he said. "The other teams in the league have a jump on us. They've already been training for a week. So we've got a lot of work to do. Defense, I want you to start on some hitting drills at the far end of the field."

"Shouldn't we warm up first?" Carlos asked. "Run a few laps before we start knocking each other around? You know, to prevent guys getting hurt." He was the Saints' safety and was concerned about injuries on the first day of practice.

"I've played a little high school ball in my time," Coach Fort said, nodding smugly. "So I know what I'm doing. Besides, we don't have time to get in shape. We have to know our plays."

Jamal eyed Coach Fort up and down. He didn't look like he had ever played football. Or that he had ever been in shape.

He looked white and puffy like the Pillsbury Doughboy.

"Offense, I want you to come with me," Coach Fort said.

Jamal joined the rest of the offensive players and followed Coach.

"To speed things up, I think you should all play the same positions as last year," he said. "Who played quarterback?"

"I was the starting QB," Darnell said, stepping forward. He stood tall and let his muscular arms hang from his broad shoulders.

"And I was the backup," said Eli, who was a lot shorter and skinnier than Darnell. "I came in if Darnell got hurt or was tired. But Darnell is your guy. He's got a great arm."

Coach Fort paced in front of the two players like he was a general inspecting his troops. "Things are going to be different this year. My quarterback has to be smart. Be able to think on his feet."

"I can do that," Darnell said. "I'm getting good marks."

Coach Fort furrowed his brow. "I think Eli might be a better starting quarterback."

"How do you know?" Darnell thrust his head forward. "You haven't even seen us play yet."

"I don't have to."

Darnell threw up his hands. "You think because I'm black and Eli's white, he's smarter? That he'd be a better quarterback?"

"I didn't say that."

"But that's what you thought," Darnell said, pointing a finger at Coach.

Coach brushed off Darnell. "What do you think, Eli? How does being the number-one quarterback sound?"

Eli's eyes widened. "I dunno, Coach. I'm not sure I'm cut out to be a starting quarterback."

"Ah, there's nothing to it," Coach said, slapping him on the back. "If Darnell can do it, you can do it."

"If you say so, Coach," Eli said, his voice cracking.

"I do." He put his hands on his hips. "And that's my final decision."

Jamal wondered if Coach had different plans for him too. He had been the best wide receiver on the Saints last year. He had caught more passes than anyone and had a good thing going with Darnell. The big quarterback knew all his pass patterns, just like when they played pickup. He'd launch the ball and Jamal would catch it almost every time. Now that Eli was going to be the starting quarterback, Jamal wasn't so sure that would keep happening.

"Let's give Eli some practice throwing the ball," Coach Fort said. "Jamal, you look like you can run. Do a buttonhook and see if Eli can hit you."

Jamal was happy Coach thought he was fast. A buttonhook was an easy pass that Eli should have been able to make. But Jamal had his doubts.

Billy snapped the ball. Eli dropped back a couple of steps, then cocked his arm. Jamal ran straight downfield for ten yards, then quickly curled around to face the passer. Eli hurled the pigskin. Jamal put out his hands. But the pass never arrived.

The ball landed a few yards short and rolled between Jamal's legs.

"Don't worry about it," Coach Fort said. "You'll complete the next one."

Eli nodded. "I'll give it my best shot."

Jamal knew Eli would give it a good try. He just wasn't sure that was good enough.

Chapter Six

"Jamal!"

His mom had her morning cup of coffee in one hand and the phone in the other. A half-eaten piece of toast sat on the table. She was racing around the apartment getting ready for work. "There's a call for you—it's McDonald's."

Jamal dashed into the kitchen from the bathroom. His mom wasn't the only one running late. He had been up past midnight playing a football game on his computer and had slept right through his alarm. He knew he should have hit the sack earlier, but he just couldn't stop. He thought video games ruled. One day he wanted to work at a big gaming company like EA Sports. For now, he was teaching himself how to write computer code. He had found a website that showed you how to build simple games and he'd already started to design his own football game. The kind you play on a smartphone. He was going to call it *Sack the Quarterback*.

Jamal had a towel wrapped around his waist. His hair was still dripping wet from the shower. He almost slipped on the smooth tiled floor in the kitchen. He picked up the phone. "Hello...Work the after school shift today?...Yes, sir...I've got football practice, but I guess I can swing it...See you then."

Jamal hung up. "Mom, can you drive me to Mickey D's this afternoon?"

"You know I can't. I'm working at Best Buy today. Besides, the car needs new brakes. The mechanic said it wasn't safe to drive until they're fixed."

Jamal rolled his eyes. "So, get them fixed."

"Do you think money grows on trees?" his mom asked, raising her eyebrows. "Brakes are expensive. Hundreds of dollars. I've got to work for weeks to save that kind of cash."

"Guess I'll have to take the bus," he pouted.

"You're not the only one, Jamal. I have to take two buses all the way across town to get to the store. But it's a good thing I work there."

"I know." Jamal nodded. "I wouldn't have a computer otherwise."

"No, you wouldn't," his mom snapped. "You're just lucky the store gave me that old laptop they found in the warehouse. They said it was so out of date no one would buy it. But it's good enough for us. It might be old, but at least it works, right?"

"Yeah, it's slow, but it still does the job," Jamal said. It was the same way he felt at the moment. "I still wish I didn't have to work this afternoon though. I'll have to miss practice."

"That's too bad, but work's just as important. And we need the money. I'm sure Coach will understand."

Jamal nodded. "He did say he wanted to help us get ahead."

Jamal snapped the chin strap on his helmet and raced onto the field. He felt bad about missing practice the day before, but it was a good thing he'd gone to work. McDonald's hadn't had enough staff, and he had been super busy making Big Macs and fries. His boss had thanked him and said he was a good employee.

He wanted to make up for not being at practice by working extra hard today. Coach Fort was already out on the fifty-yard line talking to Eli, Darnell, Billy and the rest of the offense. He was dressed in the same coaching clothes he always wore—a suit.

"Listen up," Coach Fort said. "Our passing plays aren't clicking the way they should. The quarterbacks and receivers still have to learn their pass patterns."

Jamal wasn't worried. He'd been the Saints go-to guy last season. He knew all the patterns cold.

Coach flipped the ball to Eli and said, "Let's see our number-one quarterback throw a square-out to our number-one receiver."

Jamal smiled and stepped forward. He felt good being recognized as the guy with the best hands on the team.

"Where do you think you're going, Jamal?" Coach Fort growled.

"You said the number-one receiver."

"I sure did," Coach Fort said, pointing at another player. "Malik, that means you."

"Me, Coach?"

"Yes, you."

Malik had been a backup wide receiver the year before. He wasn't as sure-handed as Jamal, and he was a step slower. Malik lined up beside Eli. He ran a square-out and cut right at ten yards. Eli hit him in the hands with a perfect spiral, but Malik dropped the ball. He ran back to the group shaking his head. "Almost had it."

"I could've caught that, Coach," Jamal said. "When do I get my chance?"

"Oh, are you still on this team?" Coach asked.

"What do you mean?"

"I didn't know if you still wanted to be a member of the Saints because you didn't show up for practice yesterday." Coach stood in front of Jamal and stared him down.

"Yeah, sorry about that."

"Sorry doesn't cut it, Jamal." Coach Fort's face turned tomato red.

"But I had to work at McDonald's."

"I have to work too. That's why I'm wearing this suit. I came here straight from the office. The office where I'm the president of a big company." He held his fat arms out wide. "But I made a commitment to this team, so I'm here. I expect the same commitment from you."

"He just missed one practice, Coach," Billy said, shrugging. "What's the big deal?"

"Yeah, we can't just leave our jobs when we want like you do," Darnell said.

Coach narrowed his eyes. "And the same goes for everyone else. Your number-one job now is playing football. Not flipping burgers at Mickey D's. You'll be doing that for the rest of your lives anyway."

Jamal clenched his jaw. He worked at McDonald's because he had to. It was a good job while he was in high school, but was he going to be doing it forever? Not a chance.

"What happens if we really can't make it?" Billy asked.

"From now on, if anyone misses a practice he's off the team. Unless you get hit by a bus crossing the street and break your leg, you better be here. If you're not, then it's game over. You're toast. It's that simple."

Jamal heard the players grumbling as they went back to their passing drill. They were all shaking their heads. "That's harsh, bro," Darnell said as he walked away.

Jamal wanted to join them but knew he should stay back with Coach Fort. He wasn't out of the doghouse yet.

Coach put his hands on his hips. "You're lucky I'm not kicking you off the team. Now go and run five laps."

"I thought you weren't going to make the players run laps."

"The real players don't have to run. Just you."

Jamal pursed his lips. He was angry and confused. He'd thought Coach Fort was on his side. That he wanted to help him get ahead. Give him an advantage. That didn't seem to be the case. But here on the field, Coach was the boss. He called all the shots. If Jamal ever wanted to play wide receiver again, he knew he had to follow orders. He left his teammates practicing in the middle of the field while he ran around it.

Chapter Seven

Jamal and Darnell cruised down the hall. They were headed for the locker room. The first game of the season was still over an hour away, but they couldn't wait. The whole school was eager for Southside to take the field. They passed a large blue-and-gold poster hung on the wall. It said *THE SAINTS WILL GO MARCHING IN!*

"Good luck, Jamal," a cute girl said, waving as she walked by.

Darnell punched Jamal lightly on the shoulder. "I wouldn't have believed that if I hadn't seen it with my own eyes."

Jamal grinned. "Playing on the Saints rocks."

He liked people knowing he was on the football team. He only hoped he was going to play. After Coach Fort had laid down the law about missing practice the other day, Jamal wasn't sure he'd see any action.

He looked down the hall. He spotted Carlos speeding straight for them. He was dodging kids left and right. "We've got to get down to the locker room," he said, out of breath.

"What's the rush?" Jamal asked.

Darnell nodded. "We've got lots of time before the game, bro."

"Something's going on," Carlos said. He turned and started taking long strides. "Let's go."

Jamal, Darnell and Carlos hurried down the hall. They dashed into the gym and pushed through the door. A big group of players was huddled around someone's locker.

"What's going on?" Jamal asked.

"It's Billy," Rico said, shaking his head. "He's quitting."

Billy Chang was emptying his locker. The stocky center took out his helmet, pads and uniform and stuffed them into a big blue duffel bag.

"You don't have to do this," Jamal said.

"Yeah, I do," Billy said sadly. "You heard Coach. If you miss just one practice, you're out."

"But you're not missing a practice, man," Rico said, trying to make a joke.

"No kidding!" Billy's eyes popped wide. "I'm missing a whole game. First game of the year. What do you think Coach will say when I tell him that?"

"His face will probably turn extra pink and pop like a giant bubble-gum balloon," Rico said.

"I know. So it's best I clear out before the game."

"What's the deal?" Jamal asked. "How come you can't play?"

"You know that small grocery store my parents run?"

"Yeah, the one in Chinatown."

"The guy who stocks the shelves is sick. They need me to fill in."

"Did you ask if you could get out of it?"

"Yeah, but my dad said no way. My mom said something worse in Chinese."

Darnell shook his head. "But you're our center. Who's going to snap the ball to Eli and me?"

"We've got lots of good players," Billy said before catching himself. He wasn't a Saint anymore. "I mean, *you've* got lots of good players." He closed his locker, slung the bag over his shoulder and started to walk away. "Tell Coach I'm sorry."

The locker room door flung open. "Sorry about what?" Coach Fort steam-rolled in, almost running into Billy. His suit jacket hung open over his belly, and his tie was loose around his thick neck.

Coach and Billy stood face-to-face in the hallway.

"Looks like you're packing it in, Billy."

"I have to, Coach. I can't play in today's game. Got to work at my parents' store."

Jamal thought Coach might give Billy a break. Especially since he was the number-one center. He should have known better.

"You're doing the right thing, Chang."

"Yes, Coach," Billy said glumly.

"I can't think of anything worse than missing the first game of the season."

"I know."

"You're letting the whole team down. And you're letting yourself down."

"I don't have a choice."

"You always have a choice," Coach said, his voice getting louder. "You can say no to your parents and yes to your team."

"I can't do that. They're my mom and dad."

"Who's more important? Your parents or your coach?"

"My parents," Billy said quickly.

"You had a real future in football." Coach pointed a stubby finger at him. "Now you're going to end up just like them—working night and day in a grocery store."

"He's just working there after school," Jamal said. "It doesn't mean he'll be there forever. Maybe one day he'll start his own business."

"Yeah, that's what they all say." Coach shook his head and laughed. "Flipping burgers, stocking shelves—it's all the same. In twenty years you'll both still be doing it."

Jamal bit his lip. He didn't want to say what he really thought. That Coach was wrong about Billy and him. That they wouldn't be flipping burgers and stocking shelves forever. But he was already in Coach's doghouse. He was down to being second-string receiver. If he ever wanted to play again, he knew he had to shut up.

Coach held up a piece of paper with names scrawled on it. He waved the list in front of the rest of the team. "I've got the starting lineup for today's game right here."

He took a pen from his pocket and drew a line through one of the names. "Chang out." He held the pen ready to scratch off another name. "Now, who else has to miss today's game?"

Chapter Eight

The air buzzed with excitement. Cheerleaders danced along both sidelines, shaking their pom-poms. The Southside band played "When the Saints Go Marching In." The stands were full of fans who had stayed after school to watch the game. Principal Campbell and Coach Kemp were just taking their seats. The TV crew from *The Sports Channel* had set up their camera next to the Saints bench. They stood ready to record all the action.

The players were pumped. The Saints in their blue and gold. The Jets in their green and white. All eyes were on the referee, who blew his whistle to start the game. Rico ran the North York kickoff back to the Saints twenty-yard line. Eli and the rest of the Saints offense took the field for the first play.

Everything looked just like it had when the Saints played the year before—except for one thing. Last year's star quarterback and receiver were still sitting on the bench.

"I don't get it," Jamal said. "Last season I started every game."

"Me too." Darnell nodded. "I hit you with passes all game long. Now look at us."

"Getting splinters from riding the pine." Jamal pounded the bench in frustration.

The Saints started the game deep in their own end. Eli was doing his best to lead the team at quarterback. He stood behind the new center and called the signals for the first play. Before today, Davey Sanchez had always been a guard, one of the big guys who protected the quarterback.

But now that Billy had been forced to quit, Davey had to step in and take over.

"This isn't going to be pretty," Jamal said, watching the game.

Eli called for the ball, and Davey snapped the pigskin between his legs. Or at least he tried to. The ball went flying past Eli and rolled into the backfield.

"Fumble!" Darnell shouted, trying to alert his teammates.

Eli raced back and fell on the bouncing pigskin. He had to make sure the Saints kept possession. Then three jumbo Jets swooped in and landed on him. The ref marked the ball. There was a loss of five yards on the play. It was second down and fifteen to go for a Saints first down.

On the second play, Eli made a handoff to Rico, who was playing halfback. He held the leather in the crook of his arm and tried sweeping around the right side. Rico had good wheels, but not good enough. *Bang!* He was met by a squadron of Jets. He was shot down after picking up only a couple yards. Now it was third down and the Saints were forced to punt. Rico picked himself up and joined Eli, Malik and Davey trotting back to the Saints sideline. Coach Fort was waiting, his hands firmly planted on his hips.

"Davey, what's with the bad snap?" Coach barked. "It's like you've never played center before."

"I haven't, Coach. Billy always played center. I wish he still was."

"Forget about him. He didn't care about our team. You shouldn't care about him."

Jamal knew nothing could be further from the truth. Billy loved playing for the Saints. At practice, he was always the first guy on the field and the last guy to leave. The other players knew he'd do anything for the team. Having to quit was killing Billy.

Coach narrowed his eyes at Davey. "We can't afford mistakes like that. See that it never happens again."

"Yes, Coach." Davey nodded.

Coach Fort's round head swiveled on his neck. "Eli! Malik! Get over here." The quarterback and receiver sprinted to his side. "They're shutting down our running game."

"What should I do?" Eli shrugged, unsure what play to call.

"Next time we get the ball, let's try a pass to Malik."

"What route should I run, Coach?" Malik asked.

"A post pattern should put you in the clear."

The Jets made a couple of first downs on running plays. That moved the ball to midfield. The Saints defense finally held when Carlos made a diving tackle and brought down the Jets tight end after a short pass. The Jets had to punt. The Saints got the ball back on their own thirty-yard line.

Eli broke the huddle and sent Malik to the far left side. Davey snapped the ball. It was perfect this time. Eli grabbed the leather and rolled to his left, looking for Malik downfield just like Coach had said. Davey and the Saints guards blocked the Jets rush, giving him time to throw. Malik raced straight, then cut in toward the far goalpost.

"He's in the open!" Coach shouted from the sideline.

Eli pulled back his arm and flung the ball. Instead of the spiral that Darnell would have thrown, the ball wobbled through the air, fluttering like a wounded duck. Malik was in the clear when the ball left Eli's fingertips, but he was covered by the time the ball finally arrived.

"Uh-oh," Jamal said, covering his eyes.

Just like in their after-school pickup game, the Jet defender leaped high in the air and intercepted Eli's pass. And he wasn't finished. He dashed down the field toward the Saints goal line. Davey, Malik and Eli all tried to tackle him, but he was jackrabbit fast. Jamal opened his eyes to see the Jets speedster dance into the Saints end zone. His teammates mobbed him. Jamal glanced at the scoreboard. It was 7-0 Jets.

Eli trudged off the field. His head was down.

"What was that?" Coach Fort yelled. "That was the dumbest pass I've ever seen."

"Tried my best, Coach."

"I thought you said you were a smart quarterback."

"I think *you* said that, Coach."

"Well, you better smarten up."

Jamal elbowed Darnell on the bench. "Here comes your chance, bro. Coach has to make a quarterback change after that play. Get ready to go in."

"You better make some passes in the second half, Eli," Coach said, shaking his head. "That's all I can say."

Jamal couldn't believe it. Coach was going to give Eli another chance and leave Darnell sitting on the bench. He shook his head. At least he'd still have company.

Chapter Nine

The Saints slumped on the bench during halftime. It had been a tough game. Everyone but Jamal and Darnell was worn out. Coach lumbered in front of the players like an angry bear.

"You guys look beat out there," he growled.

"Must be from all the laps you didn't make us run," Rico wisecracked. The other players snickered.

"I thought your kind was always in shape. Just naturally."

Our kind? Jamal wondered what Coach meant.

"But don't worry. Next practice you won't be laughing, you'll be running." Coach glared at Eli, Malik and Rico. "Our offense isn't getting the job done. That means our defense has to step up. Get the ball back for us."

The Saints took the field for the second half, and the defense must have been listening. The beefy guys on the D-line started to break through the Jets front four and put pressure on their quarterback. On one play they were able to sack him for a ten yard loss. On another, the QB panicked while being rushed. He threw before he should have, and Carlos was able to pick off the pass. That gave the ball back to the Saints just like Coach wanted.

But the Saints offense couldn't get off the ground. Every running play to Rico was piled up by Jet defenders. Every passing play Eli tried was either short for only a few yards or way off the mark. His throws to Malik and the other receiver were too high or too wide. The ball never got close enough to Malik to find out whether he could even catch a pass.

The Jets hadn't been able to score any more points in the second half. But neither had the Saints. Southside was still down by seven points—a full touchdown.

The game was now late in the fourth quarter. Jamal checked the clock. Just one minute to play. The Saints had the ball at midfield and still had a chance. They had to drive down the field and score. If not, they'd lose the game. Jamal knew Coach didn't want to start the season with a loss.

Coach Fort cupped his hands around his mouth and shouted, "Let's go!"

Eli called a handoff to Rico. He barreled straight up the middle for eight yards. On second down, Eli flipped the ball to his favorite running back again. This time Rico broke a tackle and sprinted for the sideline. He wanted to stop the clock. By the time he stepped out of bounds, he had gained twenty yards. It was an awesome run.

Jamal checked the scoreboard. The clock showed thirty-three seconds. The ball sat on the Jets twenty-seven-yard line. They were closing in.

Eli broke the huddle. He took the snap from Davey and dropped back to pass. Jamal watched Malik bolt from the line and run another post pattern toward the Jets end zone. It was a pattern Jamal had run hundreds of times before and always beaten the defenders. Malik ran as fast as he could, but he didn't have Jamal's speed. The Jets safety was all over him. Had him covered like a blanket.

"Throw the ball!" Coach yelled from the sideline.

Eli tossed the pigskin. Even though Malik was covered, Eli had no choice. He had to take the chance. There was only time left for two plays. He had to make each one count.

The ball sailed out of Eli's hands, wobbling through the air.

Coach watched the pass and grabbed his head with both hands. "Noooo!"

It wasn't anything like the perfect spiral Darnell would have thrown. Malik reached out his hands, hoping to catch it. But that was all he could do—hope. He wasn't in the clear, and the ball wasn't anywhere near him. The pass floated harmlessly ten feet over his head.

Coach Fort waved his arms on the sideline. "Time-out!"

The ref blew his whistle. Eli and Malik ran to the sideline. Coach wasn't about to wait for them. He ran onto the field. His face raged red with anger. He grabbed both players by their face masks.

"What the hell was that?" he screamed.

"Sorry, Coach," Eli said. "The ball slipped."

"You're making the Fort logo look bad! And you're making me look bad!" He yanked on Malik's face mask, sending him tumbling to the ground. "There's no way I can win this game now."

Jamal shot a look at Darnell. They leapt off the bench and ran to Coach's side.

"We can still win the game, Coach," Jamal said.

"There's only time for one play," Coach Fort said. "And these clowns will never be able to score a touchdown." He pointed at Eli and Malik, who still lay sprawled on the turf.

"We can do it," Jamal said.

Coach narrowed his eyes. "You guys have been sitting on the bench all game, where you deserve to be. What makes you think you can do what these deadbeats couldn't?"

"Because we've done it a hundred times before," Darnell said.

"Okay, get in there," Coach Fort said, crossing his beefy arms. "But it's the only chance I'm giving you. If you don't score, it's back to the bench next game."

Jamal and Darnell raced onto the field, strapping on their helmets as they ran. Jamal was worried they weren't warmed up. His legs and Darnell's arm were stone cold from sitting on the bench all afternoon. But they had to find a way.

Darnell called the last play in the huddle. "Flag to Jamal."

Jamal nodded and clapped his hands. "Let's do this."

Darnell crouched behind Davey. He signaled for the ball, and Davey snapped it cleanly. Darnell dropped back deep into the pocket. He wanted to give Jamal time to run his pattern.

Jamal dashed from the line of scrimmage. He flew down the middle of the field, straight at a Jets defender. Just when it looked like he was covered, Jamal slanted to his left. He darted toward the flag in the corner of the end zone. The Jets safety couldn't keep up. Jamal sprinted into the clear.

Darnell cocked his powerful arm and launched the ball. The pass sailed smoothly through the air. There was no wobble, no flutter. It was a perfect spiral arcing through the blue sky.

Jamal looked over his shoulder. The ball shot toward him, but he didn't slow down. His legs raced beneath him as he reached out his hands. The ball landed softly on his fingertips. He squeezed the pigskin and pulled it tight to his chest.

The referee threw both hands straight into the air and blew his whistle. Touchdown!

Darnell ran toward Jamal in the end zone. Their smiles were as wide as the field. They leaped at the same time and bumped shoulders. The rest of the Saints offense caught up and mobbed Jamal.

"We're not done yet," Jamal said.

"One point or two?" the referee asked.

Darnell held up a pair of fingers. "We'll go for two."

The Saints had scored on the final play. But they still trailed 7-6. They could just kick the ball through the goalposts for a single point and tie the game. But they had come this far. Why not go for the win?

"Huddle up," Darnell said. "Buttonhook to Jamal."

The ref placed the ball on the five-yard line. Jamal stood on the far left side, his leg muscles ready to explode when the ball was hiked. Darnell called for the snap and Jamal bolted. The Jets defender thought Jamal was going to keep running deep into the end zone just like he had done the play before. But as soon as Jamal crossed the goal line, he hooked around so that he was facing the quarterback. Darnell had already thrown the pass before Jamal turned. The two friends had practiced the play over and over again. The defender had been fooled. He had no chance to knock the ball away. The pigskin zipped into Jamal's waiting hands.

The referee's hands shot high into the air again. Two points!

Chapter Ten

"Pump it up!" Rico shouted.

Carlos rushed over to his iPod and cranked the volume. LL Cool J thumped through the speakers and into the locker room. Jamal joined the team in a giant huddle in the middle of the floor. The players were still dressed in their blue-and-gold uniforms. They all jumped and punched the air with their fists in time with the beat.

"Saints!" *Thump, thump.* "Saints!" *Thump, thump.* "Saints!"

The victory party was on.

Jamal went back to his locker. Darnell cruised over with a huge grin plastered on his face. They pounded fists.

"Just like old times," Darnell said.

"That was a sweet pass."

"That's the only kind I make." Darnell pretended to throw a ball. "And awesome catch."

"You make it easy, man. I just reached out and the ball was there. Even Malik could have caught that one." Jamal laughed and turned around. His eyes grew wide. Standing right next to him was Malik, hanging his head.

"I was just kidding." Jamal felt bad for Malik. "You're a good receiver."

"Nowhere near as good as you," Malik said, shaking his head. "If I had your moves, maybe I could have got in the open and caught that pass. I deserved what Coach did to me."

Jamal locked eyes with Malik. "No one deserves to be thrown around like Coach did to you. You were just doing your best."

Darnell nodded. "Coach was way out of line. If he had tried that on me, I would have popped him one."

"It wouldn't have happened if Jamal was in the game like he should have been," Malik said.

"And Darnell should have been at quarterback right from the opening kickoff," Eli said. He had started taking off his equipment a couple of lockers over. "His arm is like a gun. Mine is nothing but a toy pistol. I don't know what Coach sees in me."

Jamal called Eli over. "Stand beside Darnell." Eli took a few steps and stood next to the big quarterback. "Now do you see what?"

Eli looked at Darnell and then at himself. "Yeah, Darnell is a lot stronger than me."

"Any other difference between us?" Darnell asked, grinning at Eli. "Anything at all?"

"Well, you're black and I'm white."

"Bingo," Darnell said. "You noticed."

"But I don't think about that stuff."

"I know *you* don't, bro." Darnell reached out to bump fists with Eli. "But the newest member of the team does."

The locker-room door swung open. The TV cameraman and reporter pushed their way into the crowded room. Jamal knew who they were hunting for.

"Coach!" the reporter called, waving his microphone. "Got a minute to talk to us?"

"Anything for TSC," Coach Fort said, smiling for the camera. He tried to button his suit over his gut to look good but couldn't.

"Great game," the reporter said. "Were you ever worried the Saints couldn't come back and win?"

"There was never a doubt in my mind," Coach Fort said. "It was all part of the game plan."

The reporter wrinkled his brow. "So waiting until the last play of the game to win was your plan all along?"

"Yeah, I wanted to make it exciting for the fans. Build up the suspense."

Jamal and Darnell moved closer to where the reporter was interviewing Coach Fort.

"And what about replacing your quarterback and receiver?" the reporter asked. "Was that your idea too?"

"Totally my idea. I thought putting in a new QB and receiver would confuse the other team. And my plan worked."

Jamal shook his head. He couldn't believe what he was hearing. *His plan?* Without their telling Coach to put them in the game, the Saints would have lost. Coach Fort was flat-out lying.

"What about that two-point conversion? That was a gutsy call."

"You bet it was. That's how I call 'em." Coach Fort shrugged and gave a big smile for the camera. "Who wants a tie when you have a chance to win the game, right?"

"It was a great pass and catch by your new quarterback and receiver. Who are those guys?" the TSC reporter asked, scanning the room.

Jamal thought Coach would finally have to own up to who scored the touchdown.

"Names aren't important," Coach Fort said. "Besides, I called the play myself. I made it happen."

Jamal and Darnell stepped back, clenching their fists.

A big crowd had surrounded the interview. At first the players were excited to be on TV. Rico, Carlos, Eli and Malik were all hamming it up. Every time the camera panned in their direction they'd wave or make a goofy face. But by the end, they were just rolling their eyes. They wondered what game Coach had been watching. He had made it sound like the Saints were a one-man team. And that man was Coach Fort.

Chapter Eleven

The city bus stopped a couple of blocks
from Jamal's apartment building. He
stepped off and started trudging home in
the dark. He had just finished working his
regular shift at Mickey D's. The one that
started an hour after his football practice
stopped. He always showed up tired and
hungry, but the job did have some tasty
benefits. He got to eat all the food he
wanted. Tonight he had wolfed down two
Quarter Pounders and a large order of fries.

Jamal had taken the bus to work and back. His mom's car still wasn't fixed. It sat in the parking lot, unsafe to drive without new brakes. He was beat. And he still had math and socials homework to do. He wouldn't be able to work on his computer game tonight.

He walked along the sidewalk, minding his own business, but something wasn't right. He felt like he wasn't alone. Like he was being followed. Suddenly he heard the growl of an engine behind him. He looked over his shoulder. A car with lime-green paint pulled up beside him. It slowed to the same speed he was walking. The man in the front passenger seat rolled down his window. Lil Wayne thumped out. Jamal recognized the music and the face from the parking lot. The bald guy with tattoos.

"What up, bro?"

"Just going home," Jamal said. He didn't want to talk, but he thought there could be trouble if he didn't answer.

"You look tired, man."

"Long day. Had to take the bus."

"Want a job this week?"

"I got a job."

The man laughed out the window. "I mean a real job, with real money."

Jamal knew he should say no. But his mom's car needed repairs, and it was taking forever to save up for them. His mom would sure like to drive to work instead of taking the bus. And so would he.

"How much?" Jamal asked, shooting a glance at the man.

"Still ten large, kid."

Ten thousand dollars seemed like a million to Jamal. He didn't think it would hurt to find out a bit more.

"What do I have to do?"

"Nothing much," the tattooed man said. "Just load a truck."

"When?"

"Friday night. Ten bells."

"Where?"

"You'll find out. We'll pick you up in the alley behind your crib."

Jamal nodded and kept walking. The green car bounced up and started to pull away. The bald man hung out the window and said, "Make sure you're there, bro." Then he laughed again.

"I'm going out," Jamal called to his mom from the kitchen. She was in the next room, watching TV.

"It's almost ten o'clock, Jamal. Seems kind of late to be just leaving."

"It's Friday night, Mom. Things don't get going until later."

"Who are you meeting?"

"Some new guys. You don't know them."

"You should bring them over for a Coke sometime."

"Yeah right." Jamal rolled his eyes. There was no way his mom would ever let any gang members set foot in their apartment again. Not after what had happened to his dad.

"Have a good time," his mom called.

"Don't wait up for me. I might be late."

Jamal took the elevator down ten floors and slipped out the back door. The alley behind the apartment building was dark.

He heard a car start up. Two bright head-lights flashed on and off. He walked over to the car, and someone swung open a door. He got in the backseat.

"Good timing," the bald man said from the front. "What's your name, kid?"

"Jamal."

"I'm Pedro." He reached into the back-seat to bump fists. "And this is Martinez." He pointed at the driver.

The light inside the car was dim, but Jamal could see Martinez also had dragons and knives tattooed on his arms. He looked even more muscular than Pedro. Jamal checked out the back of the driver's head, only inches in front of him. He saw an *SS CREW* tattoo inked onto his neck.

"Where are we going?"

"You'll find out when we get there," Pedro said.

The lime-green Chevy drove for about twenty minutes, Eminem thumping from the speakers. Jamal knew they were on the way to do something bad. Probably steal something. He didn't even want to know.

Instead, he sat silently staring out the window. The roads looked familiar, but he couldn't remember why at first. Then it hit him. This was the way to his mom's job.

The car turned into a big parking lot in front of a shopping mall. It was the mall where his mom worked at Best Buy. Martinez cruised around the back to the alley that ran behind the stores. It was late now. Pitch black. He turned off the Chevy's lights and kept driving. The car stopped next to a truck with its back door open.

"We're here," Pedro said. "Let's move."

"But this is Best Buy," Jamal said. "There are tons of TVs and computers inside."

"And soon they're going to be inside our truck." Pedro narrowed his eyes. "You got a problem with that?"

Jamal knew he couldn't tell them not to rob his mom's store. That's what gangs did. "No, man."

"Good," Pedro said.

"What if there are security cameras?" Jamal asked.

"We'll take care of them," Pedro said, getting testy. "Now get in there and carry out all the boxes we tell you to."

Jamal followed Pedro and Martinez through the back door of the Best Buy. The door had been busted open and the alarm turned off. These guys know what they're doing, Jamal thought.

Large overhead lamps flooded the storage room with light. Pedro pointed at big cardboard boxes. Jamal helped Martinez and the truck driver start to carry the heavy boxes back to the truck. TVs, computers, monitors, tablets, cameras, phones—it was going to be a huge haul.

Suddenly, Martinez dropped a box. He tilted his head and cocked his ears. "What's that?"

Jamal stopped and listened. He heard two sirens in the distance. And they were getting closer.

"It's the heat," Pedro said. "Let's split."

Jamal watched Pedro and Martinez race into the back alley and jump into the Chevy. The engine roared.

"Let's go, man!" Pedro shouted.

Jamal was paralyzed with fear. His legs wouldn't move. He stood frozen in place.

"We can't wait for you, man!"

Jamal watched the lime-green car peel out. Tires squealed. Rubber burned. The truck bolted from the crime scene seconds later. Jamal was left alone in the dark. Finally, his legs started to work. He began sprinting down the alley. Instead of running for a pass, he was running for his life. He didn't want to get caught by the cops.

But it was too late. One police car sped toward him from the left end of the alley. Another drove toward him from the right. Red and blue flashes lit up the darkness. Sirens blared. He was trapped in the middle. Caught in the headlights. He threw up his hands. There was no way out.

A minute later he was sitting in the back of another car. This time it was black and white, with the word *Police* along its side. The squad car pulled away. He stared out the window, watching the Toronto skyline blur past. His body hunched forward. His wrists behind him, handcuffs clamped tightly around them.

Chapter Twelve

"You're under arrest for suspected theft," the police officer said. He was heavyset and dressed in a dark-blue uniform. A blue hat with a red band was pulled low on his forehead. He locked eyes with Jamal. "It's a serious crime, son. You need a lawyer."

"I don't know any lawyer," Jamal said, slowly shaking his head.

"What about your parents?"

"It's just me and my mom at home."

"Maybe you better call her."

Another policeman unlocked his handcuffs. Jamal rubbed his hands together. His wrists were sore where the metal had dug in. He was led down a hall to a phone on the wall. He stood there wondering what he was going to say. Finally, he dialed. After only one ring his mom picked up.

"Hello."

"Mom, it's me."

"Are you all right? I've been worried sick."

"Yeah. I'm okay."

"Where are you? It's the middle of the night."

"I'm...I'm in jail."

"Jamal! What for?"

"I was trying to get some money to fix the car."

"So you stole money?"

"No, I was helping some guys take some stuff from a store."

"What guys?"

"Some gang guys."

"What store?"

Jamal took a deep breath before answering. "Best Buy."

"*What?* You robbed my store? I can't believe it. If they find out you're my son, they'll probably fire me."

"I know. It was stupid."

"Can you get out?"

"The police said I need a lawyer."

"I can't afford a lawyer, Jamal. You know that."

"What am I going to do?"

"Don't worry. I'll figure something out."

"Okay, thanks."

"You've done a dumb thing, Jamal. But I still love you."

Then his mom hung up.

Steel bars stretched across the front of Jamal's cell. He sat bent over on the hard bench, his elbows resting on his knees and his head between his hands. He hadn't slept a minute since being locked up four hours before. The sound of drunks yelling and junkies swearing had kept him awake through the night. He lay on the concrete slab and closed his eyes. He wondered how long he would have to stay in jail—how long it would take his mom to find a lawyer.

Early-morning sunlight started to stream through the small window high on the wall. Jamal squinted as a policeman approached his cell.

"Wilson," the policeman said, jangling his keys. "Someone is here to get you released. You're free to go."

Jamal sat up and rubbed his eyes. He wondered who his mom could have found to come and get him out.

The metal bars clanged as the officer opened the cell door. He took Jamal by the arm and brought him out to the meeting area. Jamal's tired eyes popped wide open when he saw who it was.

"Looks like you need my help, Jamal."

"Coach, what are you doing here?"

Coach Fort stood beside a dark-haired man wearing an expensive suit. Coach had a big smile on his face. But Jamal didn't know if he could trust him. Not after he'd taken all the credit for winning the game.

"Your mom called and explained the whole situation. Said you needed a lawyer and that she had no one else to turn to. She was crying. I told her not to worry, that Coach Fort would take care of it. So here I am with my lawyer to get you out."

"But why would you do that for me?"

"I have my reasons," Coach said. "Hey, if you can't help your players when they're in trouble, who can you help?"

Jamal was confused. Coach hadn't helped any of the other players before. When Jamal had missed practice, he was benched. When Billy had to work, he was forced to quit. Coach was up to something, but Jamal didn't know what. He was too tired to care right then though. He was just happy to be out of jail.

Jamal walked toward the exit with Coach and his lawyer. He knew he had made the biggest mistake of his life. He didn't want anyone to know about it. He wanted to hide. Make it all go away.

Coach pushed through the front door of the police station. The moment the door opened to daylight, he burst into a big grin and waved.

What is going on? Then Jamal saw why Coach was so excited.

There must have been twenty reporters lining the stairs leading up to the police station. TV, radio, newspaper—they were all there. All shouting questions.

"Coach, it looks like you're bailing out more than just the Southside football program," a TV reporter said.

"That's right." Coach smiled into the camera. "Without me, most of the players would be in a gang, in jail or dead. Take this young fella standing right next to me, for example." He wrapped an arm around Jamal's shoulder. "This is one of my players on the Saints."

Jamal couldn't believe Coach was doing this on TV. He didn't want anyone to know he was a criminal. He wanted to run away, but he was surrounded by a crush of people. He couldn't move. He kept his head down and hid behind Coach as best he could.

"This player got mixed up with a gang last night, and I had to bail him out this morning. It's all in a day's work for Roland Fort and Fort Sports."

"Is that why they call you Saint Roland?" the TSC reporter asked. "Because you're saving the players?"

"Well, someone has to save them. It's not like the school is doing anything to help them. The classes aren't preparing them for any kind of career. The kids are failing everything anyway."

A reporter reached out with a microphone. "So the players on the team have no future?"

"They have no dreams. No skills. No ambition. They're going nowhere in life. They have nothing without football and me."

Coach Fort waved to signal the end of the interview. "Thanks for coming out here so early, everyone. I'm glad you all could make it. I'll see you at the next game."

Jamal stumbled down the rest of the stairs toward Coach's silver Mercedes parked on the street. He thought twice about getting into another car. Every time he did, something bad happened.

Chapter Thirteen

"I don't know what's worse," Rico said, pointing his hot dog at Jamal. "What you did or what Coach said on TV."

Jamal had kept a low profile at school all week. He'd tried to be a model student. He showed up at class on time. He did his homework. He answered questions when asked. But he was still the talk of the school, and not in a good way. Every time he walked down the hall, the other kids would turn and stare. "That's him," they'd say, then steer clear of him. There was finger pointing and whispering wherever he went. He might as well have had a sign on his back that read *SOUTHSIDE PUBLIC ENEMY NUMBER ONE*.

Carlos nodded at Jamal across the cafeteria table. "Yeah, dude. You're giving us all a bad name. Ripping off a Best Buy? That was crazy."

"I know, but we needed the money. Our car was never going to get fixed without it."

"No one needs money that bad," Darnell said, putting down his can of OJ. "All you've got to do is work a little longer."

"You could have been killed," Eli said. "The Southside Crew is bad news. They're all packing heat. You could have been shot."

"Just like your dad, bro," Darnell said.

Jamal nodded slowly. "That's what my mom said."

"Doesn't she work at a Best Buy?" Rico asked. "She must be on your case, man."

"Yeah, the cops made her ground me for three months." Jamal's shoulders slumped. "I can't go anywhere except to school, work and football. And I can't even do that this week. My mom won't let me go to practice. She cleared it with Coach Fort though."

"After seeing Coach on TV, I don't know if I even want to play football anymore," Darnell said. The big quarterback shook his head. "He thinks we're all losers."

"I couldn't believe the words coming out of his mouth at the cop shop," Malik said. "He was dissing all of us."

"I may not like going to school," Rico said, "but I'm not going to join a gang. And I'm not going to jail. Coach was dead wrong."

"He just likes being on TV," Eli said. "He likes all the attention."

Carlos agreed. "He doesn't care what happens to us. He just cares about making himself look good."

"And his stupid Fort Sports stores," Rico said. "I hate having a cartoon fort on our uniforms. I feel like ripping it off. We're the Saints, man."

Jamal glanced at his teammates around the table. "I don't know about you guys, but I don't want to play another game for that guy."

"It's not worth it," Carlos said. "Coach may have the bucks, but he has no respect."

"No, he doesn't respect us, does he?" a woman said.

Jamal turned his head to see who was talking. His eyes widened. Principal Campbell had been passing through the cafeteria. Now she was standing right behind him!

"He had a lot of nerve saying what he did," she said, glowering. "Southside is a good school. We may not have money like some of Toronto's rich schools, but we do the best we can. Our teachers work hard. We care about our students. And our students care about school. Isn't that right, Jamal?"

"Yes, ma'am."

"You'd rather be here than in jail, I presume."

"Yes, ma'am."

"And Rico," the principal said, crossing her arms, "you don't come to school just to play football, do you?"

Rico raised his eyebrows like he had been caught stealing. "No, ma'am. If I had the choice between football and math class, I'd choose math every time." He breathed a sigh of relief after telling the fib.

"So Coach Fort has it all wrong," the principal said.

"Totally," Jamal said.

"Then I'm going to have a word with him. If he's going to say bad things about Southside on the news, then I've got news for him. We don't need a coach like that."

Darnell nodded. "We don't think so either."

"I don't know what we're going to do about it though." The principal wrinkled her brow. "We have a contract. We can't fire him."

"Leave it to us, Principal Campbell," Jamal said, eyeing his teammates. "We'll take care of it."

The principal continued on her way through the noisy cafeteria. She marched quickly, like she was on a mission. Her face was stern. Her eyes looked straight ahead.

Jamal thought she might be going to her office to phone Coach Fort and give him an earful.

Rico turned to Jamal. "Sounds like you have a plan to get rid of Coach."

"Not yet, but I'm working on it."

Chapter Fourteen

Game day. The fourth tilt of the season. Southside was up against the Rexdale Rams. This was going to be the biggest game of the year so far, and not just because the Saints were facing the best team in the league. The Rams had won the championship the year before, and on top of that, Rexdale was where Coach Fort had played high school ball. He couldn't stop bragging about what a star he had been there. None of the players believed him, of course. But he was Coach and could

say what he wanted. Jamal knew he would do anything to win this game. Anything to look good in front of the TV cameras.

Today marked Jamal's first day back at football. His mom had finally agreed to let him play again. The time off had given him time to think. And plan. He cruised down the hall and stopped by Darnell's locker. The Saints quarterback had his head buried deep inside, looking for a book. Jamal tapped him on the shoulder. "Be in the locker room an hour before game time. And bring scissors. Pass it on."

Darnell pulled his head out of the locker and nodded.

Jamal walked farther down the hall. Past the computer room where he'd go to work on his video game during his spares. Past a *SLAM THE RAMS* poster the cheerleaders had painted. All the way to Rico's locker. He delivered the same urgent message to the running back. From there the news spread through the team like wildfire.

Jamal stood on a bench in the middle of the locker room. Everyone had arrived early for the secret meeting. Some had started to change into their equipment. Some were still in their jeans and T-shirts. But when Jamal started to speak, everyone stopped and listened. All eyes were on him.

"Remember when we voted to take the money from Fort Sports to start the team again?"

"That was a big mistake," Carlos said, shaking his head.

"And then we had to let Mr. Fort coach?"

"An even bigger mistake," Darnell said.

"Yeah, a big fat mistake." Rico held out his arms as wide as Coach Fort's belly.

Jamal scanned the faces in the room. "Well, it's time to take another vote."

"It's going to be different this time," Malik said, punching the air. He was still mad at being thrown around by the coach.

Jamal lifted one arm above his head. "All those in favor of getting rid of Coach Fort, raise your hand."

Every hand in the room shot up.

"So now what?" Eli asked. "We all voted against Coach Fort. But there's still one big problem."

"Yeah, how are we going to do it, bro?" Darnell asked.

Jamal smiled. "First we're going to ask him nicely to leave."

"You know he's not going to do that," Eli said, shaking his head. "What happens then?"

"Then we use plan B."

Carlos wrinkled his brow. "Plan B?"

"We're going to use our secret weapon. The one thing Coach Fort fears the most."

"What's that?" Rico kidded. "An all-you-can-eat buffet that's run out of food?"

Jamal smiled at the joke but shook his head. "Nope. We're going to make him look bad in front of the TV cameras."

Darnell held up the pair of scissors he had brought. "So what are these for?"

"Put on your uniforms and you'll find out," Jamal ordered.

The Saints suited up—blue-and-gold jerseys and pants pulled on, cleats laced up, helmets at the ready.

"All set," Darnell said, looking around the room.

Jamal motioned to the players. "I want everybody on the kickoff team over here." Rico, Carlos, Malik, Davey and the rest of the players who lined up for the opening kickoff gathered in front of him. Jamal didn't know if he and Darnell would be allowed to start the game, so they didn't include themselves.

He tossed a roll of white athletic tape to each player. The wide kind used to wrap wrists for protection. "Now, I want each player to cut pieces of tape to make a big letter and then stick the letter on the front of his jersey."

"How do we know what letter?" Rico asked.

Jamal pulled a sheet of paper from his pocket. It was a list of all the players, with a letter beside each name. He ran his finger down the page.

"Rico, you're S."

He read off the letter for each of the other players.

"You guys are going to start on offense when we get the ball. But one mistake and you're on the bench. Got it?"

"Are you sure we should be starting?" Malik asked.

Coach Fort put his hands on his hips. "Are you questioning my decision?"

"Yeah, we are," Eli said. He was tired of being threatened by Coach. "Darnell is twice the quarterback I am."

"And Jamal can outcatch me any time," Malik said. "They should be starting on offence, not us."

Coach's head bulged. Veins popped out of his neck. His eyes narrowed to slits. "Anybody else have something to say? Anybody else want to tell me how to run the team? *My* team?"

Jamal stepped forward. "That's just it, Coach. It's not *your* team—it's *our* team."

"Oh, is it?" Coach Fort asked. "Is it your twenty thousand dollars?"

"No," Jamal said, shaking his head.

"Is the equipment yours?"

"No."

"How about the uniforms?"

"I guess not."

"I didn't think so." Coach Fort pointed his thumb back at himself. "Without me, you wouldn't have a team. You wouldn't have a reason for going to this crappy school. And you wouldn't have a future. The only place you'd be going is off to join a gang. Or back to jail. So you'll do what I tell you to do. What have you got to say to that?"

Jamal stood nose to nose with Coach Fort. He glared right back at him. He wasn't afraid of his power any longer. "I'd say we don't want you to be Coach anymore."

"Weren't you listening to me?" asked Coach Fort, cupping his ear with his hand. "I own you. Now get out on that field right now before I kick you off the team."

Jamal gave a thin smile and nodded. "Okay, Coach, but don't say we didn't warn you."

The Rexdale Rams were already on the field. Their red-and-black uniforms were spread across the turf as the team warmed up. Jamal led the Saints blue-and-gold onto the gridiron to join them.

He scanned the field, searching for something as he ran. His secret weapon. He moved past the stands, where Coach Kemp sat watching the game like he always did. Jamal didn't see it. He smiled at the Saints cheerleaders dancing on the sideline. He didn't spot it there either. Finally, he approached the Southside bench and saw what he was looking for—the TV crew from *The Sports Channel*. The reporter and cameraman were setting up right beside the Saints bench.

Perfect. He smiled to himself. It was go time.

The referee blew his whistle for the players to line up for the opening kickoff.

"Kick it deep!" Coach Fort shouted from the sideline in front of the Saints bench.

Jamal nodded at the twelve members of the kickoff team. Rico, Carlos, Malik and the other nine players ran onto the field. They lined up in the same order Jamal had assigned in the locker room.

"Hey, Coach," the reporter said, pointing across the field. "What's with the letters on the uniforms?"

"What are you talking about?" Coach Fort asked. He blocked out the sun with his hand and stared at the players.

"Looks like your team has a message," the reporter said. He turned to his cameraman. "Make sure we get a closeup of what it spells."

"It doesn't spell anything," Coach Fort said, looking at the players still packed tightly together. "It's just a bunch of letters."

"Spread out!" Jamal cried.

On his command the twelve players broke into three words—the three words that Jamal hoped Coach Fort would never forget.

SACK THE COACH

"What the hell's going on?" Coach Fort yelled, throwing up his hands.

"Just a wild guess," the reporter said, "but I think your players want you fired. Looks like Coach Roland isn't a saint after all."

"Jamal!" Coach Fort screamed. "Are you behind this?"

"I warned you, Coach."

"Without me, the Saints would be nothing!" Coach Fort spat out the words.

"You've got it backward, Coach. Without the Saints, you'd be nothing."

"Turn off the camera!" Coach shouted at the reporter. He raced over and tried to cover the camera lens with his hand.

The cameraman dodged the coach and kept the camera rolling. The reporter launched into a series of rapid-fire questions, each one making Coach Fort more and more steamed.

"Get off the field!" he shouted, his arms spinning like a windmill.

"Not going to happen," Jamal said. "The players are staying in position until everybody sees our message. Until everyone knows we want you gone."

The cameraman moved right in front of Coach and zoomed in for a closeup.

"Get out of my face!" Coach shouted, pushing the camera out of the way.

"There's only one way to make it stop," Jamal said.

"What do I have to do?"

"Quit."

Coach Fort looked like he was going to explode. He grabbed both sides of his head. "All right, I quit. But don't think for a second that you've won. You may have started this war, but I'm going to finish it. Finish all of you."

Coach Fort turned and stormed off the field, his suit jacket flapping in the breeze.

The camera zeroed in on Coach as he lumbered away, then panned back to Jamal.

"We did it!" he called across the field to the players.

The Saints kickoff squad ran cheering to the sideline even before they had kicked the ball.

The Rams stood and watched. They looked confused. So did the referee. So did the crowd. No one could figure out why Southside was celebrating. The Saints were cheering like they had already won the game.

"See ya later, Coach!" Rico shouted, pumping his fist in the air.

Carlos let out a whoop. "I knew we could do it!"

"Sweet!" Malik yelled.

Jamal made a *T* with his hands. "Time-out!" he called to the referee.

"You have sixty seconds before the game starts again," the ref said. "And remember you still have to kick off."

"It's great we got rid of Coach Fort," Darnell said. "But now we've got another problem. We need another coach."

"And we need him now," Rico said.

"What's your plan for that?" Eli asked.

Jamal smiled. "Plan C coming up." He raced over to the stands. "Coach Kemp, welcome back."

Chapter Sixteen

Jamal was surrounded. The opening school bell was about to ring and half the team was still huddled around his locker.

"What a game, man!" Rico said.

"I still can't believe we won." Malik couldn't wipe the giant grin off his face.

"It doesn't get any closer than twenty-one to twenty," Davey said.

Rico held up a single finger. "One point is all it takes."

Eli turned to the winning quarterback. "That was an awesome pass, Big D."

Darnell grinned and waved him off. "It was nothing, bro. I was just doing what I do. You know, making perfect throws with just seconds to play against the best team in the league."

"It's a good thing you were playing QB and not me."

"Yeah, we can thank Coach Kemp for that," Darnell said. "It sure is good having him back."

"Anybody forgetting something?" Jamal asked.

"Like what?" Rico joked. "The guy they featured on *The Sports Channel* last night? The guy they showed beating his coverage and blazing into the end zone to make a diving catch with just one hand?"

"Yeah, that guy," Jamal said. "It was a pretty awesome catch if I do say so myself." He pounded fists with Darnell to thank him for the sweet pass.

"It wasn't quite as awesome as the

video they showed before your catch," Eli said.

"You mean Coach Fort going crazy on the sideline when he figured out our secret message?" Malik asked.

"I thought he was going to have a heart attack right on camera." Darnell pretended to be in pain, grabbing his chest with one hand.

"He sure got out of there in a hurry," Eli said.

Malik laughed. "I didn't know he could run that fast."

"Waddle is more like it," Rico kidded.

Suddenly the speakers in the hall crackled with a school announcement. "Would Jamal Wilson please report to the principal's office."

"What's going on?" Darnell asked. "You haven't been hanging with the Southside gang again, have you?"

"No way." Jamal shook his head. "I learned my lesson."

"Then what is it?"

"Beats me." He shrugged.

Carlos came flying out of an empty classroom. His eyes were wide. "I bet it has something to do with what I just saw. Look what's in front of the school."

Carlos led Jamal, Darnell and his teammates to the window in the classroom. Parked outside was a truck with two words on its side that they had hoped to never see again. *Fort Sports*.

Jamal watched three men with orange fort logos on their jackets carry large duffel bags to the back of the truck. *This can't be good*. Jamal turned and headed to Principal Campbell's office.

"Have a seat, Jamal," Principal Campbell said. She was sitting behind her big oak desk. Coach Kemp sat in one of two chairs in front of her.

Jamal stood in the doorway. His brow was wrinkled with worry.

"You can relax," the principal said, motioning him in. "You're not in trouble. In fact, I'd like to thank you for getting rid of Coach Fort. Taping a message on your uniforms was very clever."

"But we do have a problem," Coach Kemp said.

Jamal nodded.

"Mr. Fort called me this morning," Principal Campbell said. "He was madder than a hornet. He said he was taking his uniforms back."

Jamal had worried this might happen. "And the equipment?"

"Everything," Coach Kemp said. "Even the balls."

Jamal slumped in his chair. He had loved those uniforms. They'd made the Saints look like a real team. Every last player had been proud to pull on his jersey when they played.

The principal eyed Jamal. "Since you're the leader of the Saints, we wanted you to be the first to know."

"The team is going to have to use our old equipment," Coach Kemp said.

"It's pretty beat up." Jamal shook his head sadly. "The jerseys have rips in them. The pads are too small. The helmets are scratched and old. They're not like the new ones from Fort Sports. They really protected our heads from hard hits. Someone might get hurt."

"We don't have a choice," Coach Kemp said. "If we want to stay in the league, the players have to wear something."

Jamal pursed his lips and let out a long sigh.

"I asked the school board for extra money." Principal Campbell lowered her chin, then shook her head. "But they said no."

"We look like a bunch of losers," Jamal said. "The other teams are going to laugh us off the field." He stood on the fifty-yard line with the other players, waiting for practice to start. They were all wearing their old Saints uniforms. Uniforms they thought they had left behind for good. Everyone was gawking at each other.

Darnell's shoulder pads were too small for his broad shoulders. "I look like a little kid." He didn't seem nearly as big and muscular as he really was.

Rico's jersey had a big hunk missing in front where some lineman had grabbed him the year before. "At least I have some built-in air-conditioning," he joked, pointing at the gaping hole.

Davey's helmet was too tiny for his big head. "I squeezed it on, but I'm not sure I can ever take it off. I may have to wear it to class."

The rest of the uniforms were no better. They were battered and ripped, not much better than rags. Coach Kemp did his best to get the team ready for the next game against Don Mills, but the players just moped around. No one felt like running or catching or blocking or tackling. Losing the uniforms was a real drag. After winning the last game, the team had been sky high. Now they were down in the dirt.

"The uniforms aren't great, but they're all we've got," Coach Kemp said at the end of practice. "Unless any of you geniuses has a bright idea for coming up with twenty grand for new ones, we'll be wearing these for the rest of the season."

Jamal stayed behind with Darnell. He was working on a new pattern and wanted Darnell to throw a few passes to him. Even though their uniforms sucked, they had to make the best of it. The Saints still had to win one of their last two games to make the playoffs.

Darnell hiked the ball to himself and Jamal took off from the line. He ran straight for ten yards, zigged right, then zagged left and sprinted for the sideline. Darnell dropped back and fired the pigskin. It was the first time he had seen that pattern, and he missed his target by a mile. The ball went sailing over Jamal's head, landing out of bounds and rolling all the way to the parking lot. Jamal jogged over to get the ball. But someone had beaten him to it.

"Looking for this?" Pedro asked, holding the ball in his tattooed arm.

"Hand it over, man."

"Maybe we make a trade. I give you the ball if you do another job for me."

"I didn't even get paid for the last one." Jamal threw up his hands.

"If we don't get the goods, you don't get the cash."

"I'm done working for you. I'll never need money that bad."

"That's not what I hear," Pedro said. "Rumor has it you need twenty grand. Looking at your uniform, I can see why. You look lame, bro."

Darnell ran over to where Jamal stood. He narrowed his eyes. "Everything okay here?"

"Yeah, I was just leaving." Pedro smiled, showing his gold tooth. "Let me know if you change your mind. I could lend you the money." Pedro flipped the ball to Jamal and laughed. Then he turned and walked back to the lime-green Chevy hidden behind some bushes near the parking lot.

Chapter Seventeen

Jamal clanged his locker shut. He shuffled down the hall to the computer room. When he had a spare period between classes, this was his first stop. Today it was between math and socials. A few of the other players hung out there too. Sometimes he went to do his homework. Sometimes to work on his football game. And sometimes just to surf the Net. Today, all he wanted to do was chill and forget about losing the uniforms.

Darnell was already there. He was sitting at a row of computers and hardly looked up when Jamal walked in. He was too focused on what was in front of him.

Jamal slid into the seat beside him and glanced over. His eyes grew wide. Darnell was busy playing a game on his phone. "What are you doing, man?" Jamal said. He kept his voice low so the teacher at the front of the class wouldn't hear him.

"Just playing a little *Football Freakout*." Darnell's thumbs tapped the screen frantically, like he had a nervous twitch.

"You know you're not supposed to play games in here. You're supposed to be studying and stuff."

"I can't help it, bro. It's addictive."

"So have you come up with any ideas for new unis?" Jamal asked. "We're desperate."

"I know," Darnell said, still tapping. "We look like a bunch of clowns out there. The other teams aren't going to take us seriously."

"There must be something we can do to make money," Jamal said.

Darnell hit the Pause button. "I started to think about it. Came up with the usual ways to make a few extra bucks. Collecting bottles, washing cars, bake sales. I figure if we're really lucky we can make a thousand dollars."

"So we'd only be nineteen thousand short." Jamal laughed, but he knew it wasn't funny. "Might buy us a few helmets and balls, but not much more. We need a bigger idea."

Darnell's eyes darted back to his phone. He started tapping the small screen again.

"So that's it?" Jamal asked. "No more ideas?"

"Not right now. I'm too busy playing this awesome game I downloaded."

"How much?"

"Just ninety-nine cents."

"That's cheap. How can they make money charging so little?"

"Are you kidding?" Darnell asked. "Thousands of people download it all over North America. They make a ton of coin. All we need is our own game and then we'd have it made."

Suddenly a light went on in Jamal's brain. Why hadn't he thought of that before? A huge grin spread across his face. "Come over to my house tonight. Tell Rico and Carlos too."

"Are we all going to play *Football Freakout*?" Darnell asked hopefully.

"No, something better."

"Play it again!" Darnell's eyes were glued to the computer screen in Jamal's bedroom.

"It's awesome!" Carlos said.

"I can't believe you made this yourself." Rico grinned at Jamal. "You're a computer genius, man."

"I'm still working on the game," Jamal said, his fingers flying over the keyboard. "You're looking at a beta version. That means it's almost finished."

"It looks finished to me," Darnell said. "What else do you have to do?

"A bunch more coding," Jamal explained. "Things to make sure the game runs smoothly every time it's played. Don't want it to freeze or anything like that."

He clicked the Play button again. The screen showed two football teams lined up against each other. The players were simple red and blue cartoon figures. When the ball was hiked, Jamal clicked on the left and right arrow keys to rush the four defensive linemen against the quarterback. When the linemen sacked the quarterback, the game was over. It all took Jamal about ten seconds.

"Let me try," Rico said. "I bet I can sack the QB faster."

He pushed Jamal to the side. He clicked *Play* and started rushing the linemen. "This isn't so easy. I keep getting blocked." Rico finally sacked the quarterback after twenty seconds. "How did you do it faster?"

"Practice, practice, practice," Jamal said.

Rico laughed. "Yeah, but I hate practice."

"No kidding," Carlos joked. "We can see you dogging it on the field when you're supposed to be doing your drills."

"What do you call the game?" Darnell asked.

"*Sack the Quarterback*," Jamal said. "Do you like it?"

Darnell stroked his chin, thinking for a minute. "I like the sack part, but I'm not sure about the quarterback part."

Jamal wrinkled his brow. "Why not?"

"You know how there are lots of football games out there?"

"Yeah, hundreds." Jamal nodded.

"Ours needs to be different, so people will want to pay the ninety-nine cents and download it."

"Yeah, we need money and we need it fast," Rico said. "I don't know how much longer we can wear these crappy old uniforms."

"So I have an idea," Darnell said.

"Bring it on," Jamal said. "If we can make it better, let's hear it."

"What if we changed the name to *Sack the Coach*?"

"So the game would stay the same," Jamal said, nodding, "but instead of sacking the quarterback, you'd sack the coach."

"Exactly." Darnell fist-bumped with Jamal.

"Now that would be different," Rico said. "Even I'd pay money for that."

"I could change the quarterback to look like Coach Fort," Jamal said. "Dress him in a black suit that was too small for his big belly."

Carlos broke out laughing. "That'd be hilarious, dude."

"And people would know about Coach Fort getting sacked because the story has been all over the sports news," Carlos said.

"Yeah, I must have seen the video clip of him flipping out on the sideline a hundred times," Darnell said. "It's already got thousands of views on YouTube."

"So, what do you need from us?" Darnell asked.

"I need you guys to bounce," Jamal said with a smile. "I've got a long night of work ahead of me."

Chapter Eighteen

"Why is it taking so long?" Darnell asked, sitting on the bench beside Jamal. "We need some cash fast."

It was halftime during Southside's next game. The Don Mills Lions were mauling the Saints to pieces. The score was already 21–0, and it didn't look like the Lions were going to pull in their claws anytime soon. They were out for blood.

Jamal knew they should be focused on the game, but he too couldn't wait for money to start rolling in from *Sack the Coach*.

"Like I told you, it takes a while. First I had to submit the game to iTunes for them to approve it. That takes time. Then game-playing dudes have to find out it's available. Then they have to pay and download it. And then we have to wait for iTunes to collect the dough and pay us."

"I don't know if we can wait that long," Darnell said. "Nobody wants to play in these lame uniforms. That's why we're losing, bro. They're so old I bet my dad wore one when he played for Southside."

"We can still make the playoffs," Jamal said.

"But only if we win one of our last two games. And this game is toast."

"Okay, guys, let's get out there and bring it to them." Coach stood in front of the bench, wearing his Saints windbreaker and pointing to the field. "We're only down by three touchdowns."

Jamal could always count on Coach Kemp to look on the bright side. It was such a change from Coach Fort, who had always put them down. No matter how bad the score, Coach Kemp always thought the Saints could make a comeback and win. But Jamal wasn't so sure this time. Not after having their new unis taken away. Not after having to play in rags. Not after getting pummeled in the first half. Might as well be down by ten touchdowns, he thought as he ran onto the field.

The Saints took the kickoff, and Rico ran it back to their own thirty-yard line. The offense huddled together and Darnell called the play. A square out to Jamal. The players clapped their hands to break the huddle and lined up face-to-face with the Lions.

"Where did that uniform come from?" the Lion across from Jamal taunted. "The Salvation Army?"

Jamal tried to ignore the insult. But he wasn't the only one getting a cheap shot.

"Is Southside so poor you can't afford real uniforms?" a big lineman said to Darnell.

A cornerback needled Rico. "You've got so many holes in your jersey, I've got nothing to grab. It's like you're cheating."

Jamal had heard enough. When Davey hiked the ball to Darnell, Jamal shot from the line. But he didn't race downfield for a pass like he was supposed to. He sprinted straight for the Lions cornerback and knocked him down with a straight arm to the chest. The fight was on. The Lion scrambled to his feet and took a swing at Jamal. He ducked and drove his shoulder pad hard into the Lion's ribs. The two players crashed to the ground, wrestling on the turf.

They weren't the only two fighting. The rest of the Saints squared off against the Lions. Darnell's big right hand grasped the lineman by the face guard and threw him to the ground. Rico had the Don Mills cornerback in a headlock. Davey had flattened a defensive end and was sitting on him. It was an all-out war. And it was the only battle the Saints were winning.

The referee kept blowing his whistle, trying to break up the brawl, but the players weren't listening. Both teams kept wailing on each other until the two coaches ran onto the field.

"Get off him, Jamal!" Coach Kemp shouted. "And get off the field—now! Darnell! Rico! Davey! That means you too. Move it!"

After a few minutes the two coaches had managed to clear the field. Jamal, Darnell and the rest of the Saints stood on the sideline. Their uniforms were even more ripped and stained than before. The players were still angry and gasping for breath.

"Jamal and Darnell, you guys started the fight." Coach Kemp was just as mad as the players. "You're both out of the game!"

"But Coach, you should have heard what they were saying about our uniforms," Jamal said, throwing up his hands.

"I don't care. This is football. Lots of things get said. You've got to ignore it. Be tougher than that and play through it."

"What does it matter anyway?" Darnell said. "We were losing big-time."

"If you played half as hard as you fought, you might *not* be losing." Coach Kemp turned and called for the second-string quarterback and receiver. "Eli and Malik, you're in."

Jamal slumped on the bench for the rest of the second half. He knew Coach Kemp was right. He shouldn't have lost his cool. And maybe he hadn't given his best effort. But there was no denying their uniforms were an embarrassment. The Saints didn't look like they belonged in the league. If they ever wanted another victory, they had to change something. And soon.

"I hope our game starts selling real quick, Darnell."

"Me too, bro. Me too."

Chapter Nineteen

"Would Jamal Wilson please report to the office…"

"Here we go again." Jamal rolled his eyes as he listened to the voice blaring from the hallway speaker.

"What have you done this time?" Rico joked.

Darnell got in on the ribbing. "Time for your weekly meeting with the principal, bro?"

"At least it wasn't us." Carlos laughed.

"...and would Darnell Williams, Rico Bellini and Carlos Lopez join him."

"That's more like it," Jamal said smugly. "I don't know what we've done wrong, but we can all get in trouble together."

The four teammates cruised down the hall, hung a right at the water fountain and walked into the administration area. Principal Campbell stood there waiting to greet them. At least she didn't look mad, Jamal thought.

"There's someone here to talk to you," she said, opening the door to her office.

"Hey, fellas, I'm Joe Malone, a sports reporter with TSC. You might remember me from the story I was doing on Coach Fort and the Saints."

Jamal, Darnell, Rico and Carlos all nodded. They were speechless. Not because they were talking to a reporter, but because there was a TV camera pointed right at them.

"The night we aired the 'Sack the Coach' story, we had the highest viewer ratings we've ever had," Mr. Malone said, smiling.

"So when I heard you had created a game with the same name, I had to do another story. This could be big. Maybe even bigger."

"I think Mr. Malone has a few questions he'd like to ask," Principal Campbell said.

"I sure do. Let's get started." Mr. Malone held out his microphone to Jamal. "So why did you create the game?"

"Pretty simple reason. We needed a way to make some money. And fast."

"Because Coach Fort took back all the equipment he donated?"

"You got it. Jerseys, pads, helmets, balls—everything. Twenty grand's worth."

"Ouch," the reporter said. "That doesn't sound like a very saintly thing to do."

"Now we have to play in our old gear," Darnell said. "We look like a bunch of losers."

"It's embarrassing, man," Rico said. "We get no respect in the games."

"Is that what happened in your last game against Don Mills?"

"Yeah, things got a little ugly," Jamal said.

"We need new unis real bad," Carlos said. "The Saints are a proud team. We want to look it too."

Mr. Malone nodded. "Who came up with the idea for the game?"

"That's an easy one," Carlos said. "It was our man Jamal."

"He's a computer geek." Darnell slapped him on the back.

"If making a cool football game for your phone is being a geek," Jamal said with a grin, "then I guess I'm a geek."

"That's impressive," the reporter said. "Especially since Coach Fort said you were all going to end up in jail. That none of you players could do anything but play football."

"He was totally offside with that call," Jamal said, his dark eyes staring directly into the camera. He hoped Coach Fort would be watching. "We're all going to make something of ourselves. Carlos wants to open his own Mexican restaurant. He cooks a mean chicken taco. Darnell wants to be a social worker and help kids in the neighborhood. And Rico is the funniest guy I know. Maybe he'll be a stand-up comedian one day." The camera zoomed in on each boy as Jamal talked about him.

"So who came up with the name?" Mr. Malone asked. "*Sack the Coach*—it's catchy. And it really stands out from all the other football games out there."

Jamal looked at Darnell, who looked at Rico, who looked at Carlos, who looked back at Jamal. "It was a team effort."

"And how's the game doing? Are football fans downloading it? Is your bank account growing? Have you made the twenty thousand you need yet?"

Jamal hesitated. "Well, the game just came out a few days ago. People don't know about it yet. We don't have a big advertising budget like EA Sports. So we haven't really made any money."

"This story should help get the word out," Mr. Malone said. "A lot of people watch TSC. And not just in Toronto. We have a huge audience right across the country.

Online as well. When we broadcast this interview, football fans will find out about the game soon enough."

"How soon?" Jamal asked. He knew the team couldn't wait much longer.

"Real soon." Mr. Malone smiled. "Tonight."

"Jamal!" screamed his mom. "Get in here quick!"

Jamal shot out of his room like a cannon. He had been doing homework, but he was worried something had happened to his mom. An accident. An injury. Maybe she had fallen and hurt herself. He raced into the living room expecting the worst.

"There's my handsome boy." She was sitting on the couch and pointing at the TV. There was an ear-to-ear grin on her face.

"So you're not hurt. You don't have a broken leg or anything?"

"No, why would you think that?"

"You don't usually scream at home."

"That's because I don't usually see my boy being interviewed on *The Sports Channel*. Why didn't you tell me you'd be on?"

"Because I didn't want you to get all excited and freak out."

"Who, me? You know that would never happen!"

"No. Never."

"And there's Darnell and Rico and Carlos. All you guys on TV. This is going to make you famous."

"We don't want to be famous. We want *our game* to be famous. We need people to start buying *Sack the Coach*. We can't play another game using rags for uniforms."

His mom grabbed the remote and turned up the volume.

"So remember, football fans," the reporter said, "make sure you download *Sack the Coach*." He held the screen on his phone up close to the camera to show a cartoon player chasing a coach around the field. "For only ninety-nine cents you can help Southside get some new uniforms.

It's a great game for a great cause. I'm Joe Malone, and that's my call."

"That was like free advertising for your game, Jamal."

"Yeah, pretty awesome," he said, heading back to his room. "I just wonder if anyone else watched it besides us."

He tried doing his math homework again, but he couldn't focus. The only numbers he was interested in were the ones adding up in his account, ninety-nine cents at a time.

Chapter Twenty

Coach Kemp blew his whistle. "Let's hit the showers."

He had just put Southside through another long practice. He had to make it tough to get the team ready for the next game. The Saints had to win. If they didn't come away with a victory, they could kiss the playoffs goodbye. The clock was ticking.

"We only have a week to get ready for the next game, against the Etobicoke Knights," Coach said, striding off the field.

"After what happened last week, that's going to be a challenge."

"I think there's a bigger challenge, Coach." Jamal took off his old, scratched-up helmet. "We have even less time to come up with the money for new uniforms. I don't know if the guys can play one more game without them."

"You got that right." Carlos pulled off his ripped jersey and threw it into his locker. "Everything's falling apart."

"I saw you on TSC a couple of nights ago," Coach Kemp said. "You guys looked good on TV."

"Yeah, the camera loves me," Rico joked. "I'm thinking of going to Hollywood."

"The video game looked good too," Coach said. "I even paid the ninety-nine cents and downloaded it."

"Well, at least we know *Sack the Coach* made one dollar," Darnell said. "Just twenty thousand more downloads like that and we've got it made."

"That's a ton," Rico said. "Sounds impossible."

"How do we know if there's been more than one?" Carlos asked.

"I can find out," Jamal said. "There's an app that can track how our game is selling."

"Then what are we waiting for?" Carlos asked. "Let's check it, dude."

"But I need to get online. And I don't have a phone."

"Just give me a minute," Coach Kemp said, disappearing around the corner. He came back a minute later carrying a silver laptop. "It's all yours."

Jamal set the computer on the bench and went to work. In just a few seconds he had downloaded the app and keyed in the code for their game. Suddenly the screen was filled with numbers and colored boxes.

Darnell wrinkled his brow. "Looks like a bunch of charts and graphs."

"That's exactly what it is," Jamal said. "Each one tells us how *Sack the Coach* is doing."

News that Jamal was checking out the game spread through the locker room. Eli, Malik, Davey and the rest of the team

144

huddled around the laptop. Most of the players still had their raggedy equipment on. They all had their fingers crossed. Everyone hoped they could start thinking about new uniforms.

"So what does that chart tell us?" Darnell pointed to a green box with a bunch of numbers.

Jamal focused on the screen. "That list shows how many times the game has been downloaded since it came out three days ago."

"How many?" Carlos asked. "Five or ten?"

"More like five or ten...thousand!" A huge smile spread across Jamal's face.

"Quit fooling around, man," Rico said. "This is serious business."

"I'm not kidding. *Sack the Coach* has been downloaded over ten thousand times in the last three days."

"That's what I'm talking about!" Carlos said, his eyes popping wide.

"This blue chart shows where it's been downloaded. Ontario, Alberta, British Columbia, Texas, California, New York...

pretty much all ten provinces and all fifty states. There are even some in Australia, England and China."

"It's a worldwide hit, man!" Rico shouted.

"Now the big question," Darnell asked. "How much money have we made?"

Jamal ran his finger along the screen to where it said *Total*. "Ten."

"Only ten dollars?" Rico wrinkled his brow. "I thought it'd be more."

"You've got to do more math homework," Jamal said. "How about ten *thousand* dollars!"

The big huddle around the screen erupted. There was a volcano blast of cheers. Fists pumped the air. Knuckles were bumped.

"And that's after only three days. After a week we should have over twenty thousand. And you know what that means?"

"New unis!" Carlos shouted, throwing his old jersey on the floor.

The huddle picked up the victory cry and started chanting. "New unis! New unis! New unis!"

Suddenly there was a knock on the locker-room door. Rico ran over and swung it open. Jamal was shocked to see who it was.

"I could hear the cheering all the way to my office," Principal Campbell said. "I came to find out what all the excitement is about."

"Looks like *Sack the Coach* is going to make enough money for new uniforms," Coach Kemp said.

The players exploded again. "New unis! New unis! New unis!"

"That's the best news I've heard all day," the principal said. "Maybe all year."

Coach Kemp nodded. "With your permission, I'd like to order the team new uniforms."

"Permission granted!"

For the second time in less than a week, Jamal saw Principal Campbell with a look he rarely saw—a huge smile.

Chapter Twenty-One

"Listen up!" Coach Kemp cast his eyes around the locker room at the sea of new uniforms. "I've got a couple announcements."

Jamal had just finished pulling on his new team colors. A blue jersey with bright gold numbers. Blue pants with gold stripes down both legs. And a shiny blue helmet with a big gold *S* on the side. The gear was awesome. All fresh out of the box, still with that new-uniform smell. A big shipment had just arrived at the school that morning.

The team had rushed down to the locker room early and dived in.

He glanced in the mirror. The ragtag player he used to see was gone. Now the player with the coolest uniform in the league stared back. And there was no goofy fort to be seen. He gave a silent nod and turned his attention to the coach.

"This is a big game," Coach Kemp said. "The biggest of the season. Win and we go to the playoffs. Lose and we fall short of our goal. You've had a tough year. A coach who didn't believe in you, uniforms that were in tatters, spirits that were broken." He scanned the room again. There wasn't a sound. An army of blue and gold stood at attention. All eyes were front and center. "But it's what you do in the end that counts. How you rise above the tough times that will be remembered. We can win this game against Etobicoke. Make no mistake—the Knights will give us everything we can handle. But if we work together, if we play as a team, we can bring victory to the Saints."

The team chanted, "Saints! Saints! Saints!"

149

"What's second, Coach?" Rico asked.

Coach Kemp frowned. "Davey Sanchez won't be playing center today."

"Why not?" Rico shot a glance at Davey, who was also puzzled by the announcement. "He looks fine to me, Coach."

"That's because Billy Chang will be," Coach said with a big grin. "I asked him if he was ready to play, and he said yes."

Right at that second Billy walked into the locker room. He was already dressed in a new Saints uniform.

"Where have you been hiding?" Jamal asked.

"I've been waiting in Coach's office. We wanted to surprise you guys. Get everyone pumped."

"Well, it worked," Darnell said, bumping fists. "I can't wait for you to snap the ball to me like old times."

"And don't worry about Davey," Coach said. "He'll be playing guard just like he used to."

The Saints charged onto the field. Flashes of blue and gold streaked across the green grass.

Southside was on fire right from the opening kick. On the very first play, Darnell took the snap from Billy and dropped back to pass. Jamal sprinted from his own thirty-yard line and darted across the middle of the field. Darnell flicked his wrist and hit him on the quick slant. Jamal hauled the ball in, and his legs did the rest. He broke wide around the cornerback, and then it was a foot race to the end zone. But it was no contest. Once Jamal put his powerful engine into high gear, there was no stopping him. The Knights safety was the last man to beat. Jamal cut inside of him at the last second and ran across the goal line.

The referee raised both arms high over his head and blew his whistle. The game was less than a minute old and the Saints were already ahead by a touchdown.

Jamal dashed to the sideline, getting high fives from the defensive squad as they hustled onto the field.

"This is going to be easy, dude," Carlos said as he passed.

Jamal had played too many games to think the Knights were going to fold. He knew the team in the silver uniforms would come back fighting. This game was far from over.

He was right. For the rest of the first half, the Knights offense pounded the Saints. Their quarterback was in total control. Twice Jamal watched him march his silver machine down the field and score. He mixed up his plays like a magician, so the Saints never knew what was coming next. A running sweep to the left on one play. First down. A square-out pass the next. First down. They seemed unstoppable. No matter what the call, the Knights offense sliced through the Saints defense like a knife through butter.

The referee blew his whistle to end the first half. Jamal looked over at the scoreboard and shook his head. Knights 14–Saints 7.

Chapter Twenty-Two

The Saints huddled around Coach Kemp on the sideline. He looked more disappointed than mad. "What's going on out there?" he asked, eyes moving from player to player until finally landing on Jamal.

"I thought we'd be winning," Jamal said, shaking his head. "That all we had to do was wear our new uniforms. I thought that would be enough. But they only make us *look* better, not *play* better."

Coach Kemp nodded at the team and said, "Do uniforms make you run faster?"

"No, Coach," the players said together.

"Do uniforms make you tackle harder?"

"No, Coach."

"What can new uniforms do then?

"Make us proud, Coach."

"Now we're getting somewhere," Coach Kemp said. "And can pride make you run faster and tackle harder?"

"You know it can, Coach."

"Then let's play the second half like we know the blue and gold can!"

"Yes, Coach!"

Coach was right, thought Jamal. The team had spent weeks thinking that their ticket to winning was inside a box of new uniforms. But the truth was that it was inside them all along.

The Saints were pumped. So were the Knights. The play seesawed back and forth, with the two teams giving everything they had. Muscles flexed. Adrenaline flowed. Bruising tackles were made. At the end of the third quarter, the blue and gold finally broke through. Darnell led the Saints offense into Knights territory. He threaded the needle to Jamal with a buttonhook pass. Then he handed off the pigskin to Rico on a draw up the middle. The two plays gained over thirty yards.

The Saints were on the move. Now they were on the Knights twenty-yard line. In the red zone. On first down, Darnell scrambled back into the pocket and fired a rope to Jamal, who was streaking for the end zone. He leaped high and grabbed the ball while diving across the goal line. Touchdown! High fives! The game was tied 14–14.

The Knights came roaring back in the fourth quarter. With only five minutes left in the game, their star quarterback drove into Saints territory again. He was throwing on almost every play. His arm was like a rifle. Every pass a silver bullet. Square out to his wide receiver for ten yards. Slant to his tight end for fifteen. Despite some crunching tackles by Carlos and the rest of the defense, the Saints couldn't stop the drive. They couldn't get to the quarterback.

After watching three straight first downs, Coach Kemp had seen enough.

"Time-out!"

The referee blew his whistle. Carlos sprinted to the sideline. Coach waved over Jamal to join them.

"We need a quarterback sack," Carlos said, gasping for breath. "But no one can get to him."

Jamal locked eyes with Carlos. "How did we sack Coach Fort?"

"It took all twelve guys on the field. It took a gang tackle."

"Then that's what it's going to take," Jamal said.

Coach Kemp nodded. "Full team blitz on the next play."

"You got it," Carlos said, running back to the huddle.

Jamal stood with Coach and watched the next play unfold.

The Saints lined up helmet to helmet across from the Knights. Carlos crept closer to the line of scrimmage as the quarterback called his signals. So did his safety, cornerback and linebacker teammates. Soon all twelve Saints were on the line—all ready to charge. The moment the ball was snapped, a blur of blue and gold rushed the quarterback. The Knights offensive line was overwhelmed. They couldn't hold back the Saints any longer. The dam had burst.

Carlos broke through the blocks and had the quarterback in his sights. He tried to scramble away, but Carlos tracked him down. First he grabbed him by the legs. Then a second, a third and a fourth Saint piled on, bringing him crashing to the ground. There was no escape. The Knights quarterback had been gang-tackled ten yards behind the line.

"Sack attack!" Jamal shouted from the sideline.

Coach Kemp cupped his hands around his mouth. "One more!"

The Saints defense stuffed the next play as well. A pass over the middle only gained five yards. It was third down, and the Knights' drive was grounded. Silver would have to punt.

The clock ticked down. There was under a minute, enough time for two plays. The Saints ran the kick back to midfield, and Darnell called a pitch to Rico on the right side. The speedy halfback tucked the ball in the crook of his arm and raced to the far sideline. He ran out of bounds after picking up twenty yards. The ball was at the Knights thirty-five. One play left. A touchdown would win it.

Darnell took the snap from Billy. He stepped back into the pocket, and Jamal bolted from the line. He dashed straight at the Knights safety. He faked right, then cut to the outside and sprinted for the flag in the corner of the end zone. Now it was a race. Jamal flew across the turf like a jet. The Knights defender tried to keep up but couldn't. Jamal was in the clear. Darnell pulled his arm back like a bow and threw. The ball shot through the sky like an arrow and Jamal reached out his arms. The brown leather hit his hands. He squeezed the ball tight, then tumbled to the turf in the end zone.

Chapter Twenty-Three

The music was cranked. The locker room thumped. The players shouted, hollered and cheered. Jamal had never pounded so many fists. His cheeks were getting sore from the big grin he couldn't wipe off his face. The Saints had done it. Final score 21–14. The blue and gold were in the playoffs.

"Sweet catch, bro," Darnell said from the locker next to Jamal's. "You've got the best hands in the league."

"You got me the ball." Jamal nodded at the big quarterback.

"And since I snapped the ball," Billy joked, "you can thank me."

Jamal high-fived the stocky center.

"I never could have made that grab," Malik said, dropping his helmet by mistake. "See what I mean?"

Carlos held up one of his taped fingers. "We're going all the way this year, dude."

"Yeah, all the way to the nearest Taco Bell," Rico kidded. "I've seen you eat, man."

Jamal spied Coach Kemp snaking through the crowd toward him. There was so much noise, he leaned in to speak. "There's someone here to see you. A man from the University of Toronto. He's waiting outside."

"Who do you think it is, Coach?"

"Could be a scout from their football team. He might want to offer you a scholarship for next year. This could be your big chance, Jamal." Coach Kemp smiled and patted him on the back.

Jamal zigzagged through the players to the front of the locker room. He opened the door and saw a man waiting in the hall. Jamal didn't think he looked much like a football scout. He was short and skinny and wore thick-rimmed glasses. Instead of wearing a suit he was dressed in jeans and a T-shirt. "Jamal Wilson?"

"That's me."

"I'm John Flynn from the University of Toronto."

Coach was right! Mr. Flynn must have been impressed by my touchdown catch. "So you're from the football team?"

The man laughed. "No, I don't know much about football."

Jamal's face fell. He was hoping for a football scholarship. He couldn't afford to go to university next year without one. He wondered who the man was.

"I'm from the department of computer science."

"Uh-huh. So why are you here to see me?"

"We saw the story on TV about *Sack the Coach*. It's not every day a high school student comes out with a hit computer game."

"Thanks." Jamal nodded, still not knowing why the man wanted to talk to him.

"We're very impressed and want to offer you a scholarship."

"You're kidding."

"No, we're very serious. It would be a real pleasure to have such an outstanding student join our computer science department." Mr. Flynn offered his hand. "Do you think you might be interested?"

Jamal thought back to Coach Fort. How he didn't think Jamal or any of his teammates would make it out of Southside. How they would all end up in a gang or in jail or dead. Now he could prove him wrong.

Jamal smiled and reached out. Not just to shake hands, but for something even better. His future.

Eric Howling is an advertising creative director and author of the sports novels *Head Hunter*, *Red Zone Rivals*, *Hoop Magic*, *Kayak Combat* and *Drive*. His books have been shortlisted for the Hackmatack Children's Choice Book Award, named on *Resource Links* Year's Best and picked as Canadian Children's Book Centre Best Books selections. Eric lives and plays sports in Calgary, Alberta. For more information, visit www.erichowlingbooks.com.

Titles in the Series

orca sports

orca sports

For more information on all the books
in the Orca Sports series, please visit
www.orcabook.com.